Demon Fire

Chris Cumbie

Demon Fire

Redemption

*To Jennifer,
I hope you enjoy the book!

Chris Cumbie*

Published 2018

Demon Fire
Copyright © 2018 Chris Cumbie
All rights reserved.

No parts of this publication may be reproduced, stored in a retrieval system, or transmitted in any form or by any means, electronic, mechanical, photocopying, recording, or otherwise, without the prior written permission of the copyright owner.

This book is sold subject to the condition that it shall not, by way of trade or otherwise, be lent, resold, hired out, or otherwise circulated without the publisher's prior consent in any form of binding or cover other than that in which it is published and without a similar condition including this condition being imposed on the subsequent purchaser. Under no circumstances may any part of this book be photocopied for resale.

This is a work of fiction. Any similarity between the characters and situations within its pages and places or persons, living or dead, is unintentional and co-incidental.

Cover Photography licensed through ergonomal – Shutterstock.com.

Interior art licensed through Nortnik – Etsy.com.

Interior art licensed through Dmitry – Shutterstock.com.

Printed in the United States of America

ISBN – 13: 978-1985034549

ISBN – 10: 1985034549

First Edition

Available in paperback and e-book.

This book is dedicated to my wife who has supported and encouraged me throughout its writing.

Acknowledgements

Acknowledgement and thanks to my entire family who have supported me and always encourage me in everything I do. Special thanks to the following:

Tamantha Cumbie
Hope Hendrix
Héloïse Corbeel
Linda Cumbie
Aubin Cumbie
Tim Meacham
Robin Meacham

Special editing thanks to Jane Thompson

Contents

Chapter		Page
1	A Tragic Beginning	1
2	Burn Patterns	15
3	Reflections	45
4	A Colonial Life	59
5	Awakenings	81
6	Flash Point	101
7	Radiant Heat	117
8	The Fire Within	133
9	Kindling	159
10	Outside the Box	185
11	Point of Origin	207
12	Flames of Freedom	229
13	A Burning Vengeance	265
14	Embers	279

Chapter 1

A Tragic Beginning

Demon Fire

John Taylor and his son Cole pulled into the driveway of the Talbot Lake cabin on the warmest, brightest, most perfect day of spring. Out of all the weekends and special days the two spent together, this outing to the rental by the lake was shaping up to be the best in a long time.

The two-story cabin included two bedrooms with one and a half baths on a raised patch of ground overlooking the lake. The area contained other cabins and campsites although none were close by. Plans for the evening included unpacking, settling in and grabbing a quick bite before heading outside to watch the sun go down over the water. The description of the setting sun was one of the biggest selling points to John. The brochure described it as a brilliant sky of every bright color imaginable glistening on top of the water and cascading across the tips of evergreen trees so large and tall that it seemed the Earth and Sun were reaching to meet. As they sat by the shore enjoying the view, John determined that the brochure fell short of describing the sight of the ending day. The day that would be the last the father and son would spend together.

Cole Taylor lived with his mother Janet, but maintained a good relationship with his dad. The divorce between his parents was not pleasant. There were the fights and the lawyers and the usual mess that takes place. For Cole's sake, however, this all happened at a young age, and despite the busy schedule of both parents, each was glad to share their available time with him.

Being a ten year old boy meant that among other things, Cole was growing up. He was just on the outskirts of puberty but not yet ready to leave childhood. He knew what girls were but didn't really know what to do with them. School and sports ruled Cole's world and in both subjects he excelled. One part of childhood he had not yet left behind was his love of bedtime stories. Not the kind that had little bears or leprechauns or fairies and such, but stories of sports heroes, knights on horseback, and race car drivers. Cole's mother had many talents, but story telling was not one of them so that task usually waited for dad.

On this particular night at Talbot Lake, Cole crawled into bed and John embarked on a tale about a basketball

Demon Fire

player who won the state championship against all odds. This particular story began when the sports hero was a child and it told of how the youngster grew up in poverty and fought his way through high school by playing ball. Cole loved the tale, but before the star took the first shot at the big game, he was sound asleep.

The spark was unimpressive. Then again, how impressive can a little spark be? One tiny bit of energy release which causes one little ray of light and emits a small burst of heat. Billions upon billions of small sparks occur around the world daily. From static electricity to metal on metal friction, the causes of these bits of energy are endless. In an instant it's there - in an instant it's gone, never to be heard from again. That is unless that spark happens to be in just the right place and in just the right environment, and at just the right time to heat the surrounding area enough to cause another little burst of energy - which begins a cascading effect of power that builds to the moment where enough heat is generated to start a fire.

To describe fire is to say it's alive. It eats, it sleeps, it breathes and it grows until it is stopped. Fire can be characterized as a parasite feeding off the destruction of its environment, and tonight a parasite is born. A parasite that is hungry. A parasite that will feed.

Chris Cumbie

The fire grew out of the corner of the upstairs bathroom, and seemed well pleased with its surroundings. Curtains, toilet paper, cotton swabs and cabinets, everything it could have asked for was available. Flames lifted, searching for more oxygen and more fuel to give it the needed energy to grow. The fire rolled up and across the ceiling, then crept down the other side while the temperature passed a thousand degrees. All the organic material was breaking down into burnable fumes of gas, and in less than a minute the entire room reached temperatures great enough to ignite. As the immediate area burned, however, it began losing its usefulness to the fire.

The flames now searched for more. Some way out of the confined space. Somewhere it might grow further. Blocked by floors, ceilings, walls and doors the flames were using up the very oxygen needed to keep them alive. Then, in an instant, the search ended as the fire found what it was looking for. Beside the sink, about three feet off the floor was a hole the size of a softball. Possibly overlooked by the construction manager, this opening was in the sheetrock of the bathroom and traveled straight through the wall which gave the fire a path toward another feeding ground, Cole's bedroom.

Demon Fire

It was the bottom of the ninth inning, and Cole was not having a great game. Two ground-outs and one strikeout so far. The game didn't have a great deal of importance since it was only the second week of the season, but Cole was in a position to be the hero.

His team was down by one run, and he was at the plate with one on base. Cole took in every aspect of the moment as he tapped his feet with the end of the bat and dug his cleats into the dry dirt. The smells, the sounds; Cole's time to shine was upon him. He knew the ball was about to leave his bat and go straight over the left field wall to win the game. He bent slightly at the knees, gave a few practice swings and waited for the pitch. A fastball, Cole knew it would be, screamed toward the outside corner of the plate but never made it. With one mighty swing Cole sent it over the left field wall right where he knew it would go.

The run Cole broke into turned to a trot before he got to first. Rounding the bases, he looked up at the adoring fans cheering him on. The stadium lights beamed down on Cole's greatest moment as a grin ran across his face, and little beads of sweat appeared on his brow. When he passed second, he noticed the light was growing with intensity as the liquid coming from his pores became more pronounced. Closing in on third, a flushed feeling came over him as his body became much too warm. He couldn't be getting sick, not now, not here. As he rounded the base, the sounds surrounding him changed. The crowd's cheers turned into crackling noises as the heat began to cause pain. His breathing became increasingly difficult, and Cole was about to the point of panic when, with home plate in sight, he awoke.

The smoke in Cole's room was lowering toward the bed and the heat lowered with it. Cole felt his skin burning, and although he was terrified and could barely breathe, he thought there was time, he just had to move.

After a late-night movie, John fell asleep on the living room couch. For the past month he had planned this trip. He had picked out the best cabin on the lake. He had looked at the website pictures and brochures of the place for days, and he had gone to bed each evening thinking about his and Cole's weekend together. But, being startled awake in a new location by a blood-curdling scream threw his mind for a loop.

At first John didn't know where he was or where the scream came from. The disorientation only lasted a few seconds, however, before he realized he was at the cabin and the shout was coming from the upstairs bedroom - Cole's room. This comprehension coincided with a second noise. This sound was not a scream, and it was not from

Demon Fire

Cole. It was deeper, louder and if John had more time to think about it, he would have thought it a bit sinister. But, there was no time to linger on the idea, and it left his mind as he raced up the stairs and noticed the first hint of smoke.

As Cole fell to the floor of the bedroom, he instinctively got as low as possible away from the descending heat and smoke and began crawling to the door as he let out a bellowing scream for his father. As he continued to crawl, he felt there was enough time to escape, but the fire had other plans, and as Cole lifted his body to reach the handle, the super-heated flames traversed the ceiling and traveled down to meet him.

There is a natural fear of fire. The flames, the heat and the burning of flesh bring ideas of suffering and pain that is enough to keep people up at night. Death from the actual flames is rare, however, since the toxic gases that form from the various burning materials cause most deaths. These gases are commonly referred to as smoke, and they originate from wood, paper and petroleum-based products. Smoke rises and flows along the ceiling moving out and then back down the walls toward the floor until it finds an unwilling victim to breathe it in. The heat, searing the victim's airway as it passes, consumes any remaining oxygen left in the body as it suffocates and ultimately kills.

This in fact is what happened to Cole, and as sad as it was, and as painful as it would be to his loved ones, Cole's death was the lesser of the two possible fates that night, because the fire was merely a means of transportation for a passenger who had been waiting a long time for freedom. This freedom had been gained but was only temporary since the fire would extinguish in time. The fuel would run out, and the freedom-ride would end. The passenger had been a prisoner. For how long he did not know but long enough for him not to squander this chance at a way out. He carried no luggage save for his thoughts, his feelings and his name. The name "David" that his sweet and beautiful mother had given him countless years ago.

David had found his next mode of transportation asleep in bed. A faint smile crossed Coles' face as the sweat beaded up on his forehead from the heat of the room. The transfer was close at hand but just as the flames were within reach, out of the bed Cole darted. Fear and fury overtook care and caution as the fire burned out of control pushing out in every direction trying to find its mark, but as Cole scampered across the floor David had a lapse in judgment. The flames had increased to the point where most of the smoke rushed down the walls and had gotten to Cole first. A lifeless shell was all that was left, and a cadaver served no use.

Demon Fire

Confusion and anger followed. Untold years had passed by while David lay in wait for the perfect moment when everything would come together. The area of habitation was only a small plot of land. His own little private hell that he needed help to escape. How much time had he spent there waiting, wondering if it would ever be inhabited again? Yes the occasional human would traipse across this most wretched spot, but the spark had never come. The campfires were always built too far away. The now and again lightning strike was always in the distance. Yet after all those years hope had arrived in the form of a building. A building built for the sole purpose of habitation.

David was unfamiliar with the details. He had never recalled such a structure in his past. The wooden shell was somewhat familiar, but the adornments, noise producing objects and illumination sources were alien to him. The uncertainty he might have had was soon overshadowed by the shear excitement of what the newness brought, however. It was heat. Wonderful life redeeming energy. David could feel the heat, hear it and even seemingly taste it. The type of energy that might, with the right combination of fuel and oxygen and luck, provide him with the spark he needed. His new little slice of heaven in an otherwise excruciating hell would attract the vessels he needed to escape. David would only have to wait. The heat would eventually break through its well intentioned insulators and escape. That was the plan, and it should not have taken long - but it did.

The people came, but they never stayed more than a few nights at a time, and sometimes no one came at all. Another issue was the way people acted around fire. David remembered times when open flames were a part of life. Flammable liquids were used frequently, and care was not always taken with them. A knocked over lantern, a wayward ember from the fireplace. So many fire opportunities existed then but now - nothing. The visitors never provided a flame suitable for his purpose - a flame with enough heat to transfer his energy. So again he waited. Waited for this moment. The moment that Cole lay sleeping in bed. The moment that the spark came. The moment that the flame grew. Everything in place. Everything perfect - except the boy died!

David was filled with hate and anguish. Another chance might never arise. The structure would burn and once consumed there would be nothing left, and no one would come. No heat, no flame, only decades of more nothingness. It was unbearable. David let out a scream, and although he had no vocal cords, a sound emanated from the fire. A harsh metallic noise that might not be recognizable but was vicious in its volume and sorrow. Then just before all hope was lost, a voice from below screamed out a name. The voice was frantic, and David's hope began to build again. The screams were getting closer. Someone was coming for the boy, and this time failure would not be an option.

Chris Cumbie

Chapter 2
Burn Patterns

Chris Cumbie

Demon Fire

"Hello". Jake muttered as he fumbled to put the phone to his ear.

"Jake! Oh my God, Jake!"

The voice, though quivering, was unmistakably that of Marie Forbus the lead dispatcher at the 911 communications office. Marie had a voice anyone could recognize. She had been receiving and dispatching emergency calls for Deer Creek County for over twenty years, and she always kept cool during stressful situations. Tonight , however, was different.

"Marie, just calm down and tell me what's the matter."

"I, I, I just can't believe it." Marie was nearly in tears.

"You have to tell me what's wrong. Calm down and talk slow."

"Okay." Marie sobbed, the tears now streaming down her face. "It's Chief Taylor… Up at Talbot Lake… There's been a fire… His son Cole is dead."

"I'm on my way." Jake said.

Ten minutes later Jake Landers' department-issued SUV topped eighty miles an hour as it raced down the narrow two-lane road toward the lake.

John Taylor had been the Chief of the Deer Creek Fire Department for the past eighteen years. Jake still remembers the day Chief Taylor brought him into the office over a decade ago and offered him a job. A firefighter was all Jake had ever wanted to be, and he had never forgotten the chance he was given to fulfill that dream. A flurry of emotions ran through his mind as the flashes from his red and blue emergency lights lit up the road ahead.

Jake had worked many fire scenes, both as a firefighter, then as the lead fire investigator for the county, and he had seen his fair share of bad calls. But none were this emotional. Losing people to fire was disturbing. Losing a child was beyond terrible, but losing this child in particular would affect the entire department, and everyone, including him, would suffer because of this tragedy.

Tonight would be difficult for a reason that set him apart from the other firefighters though. By the time he got to the scene, the crews would have the fire extinguished and would be finishing the clean-up operations. They would then need to deal with the emotions of the evening, but at least their work would be complete. Jake's work, on the contrary, would have just begun.

As the lead investigator for the department, Jake was called out to investigate certain incidents. If a fire was suspicious, if the property destroyed made up a high dollar loss or in the case of a fatality, Jake would be summoned. At these fires he was tasked with determining where the fire began as well as how it started. If a fire was determined to be accidental or natural in origin a report would be written stating as much, and the investigation would end. If he determined it to be intentionally set, however, a criminal investigation would begin. Jake had been cross-trained in law enforcement and deputized by the Sheriff's Office so he took a lead role in every aspect of the investigation from cause and origin, to arrest and then prosecution.

A good investigator always began with the assumption that a fire was caused by an act of nature or by accidental means. Using this method, the first action would be to find that accidental cause. Only after the non-intentional theory was disproven would Jake let himself think a fire might have been set on purpose. Having an unprejudiced mind served him well, and when a fire was found to be deliberately set, Jake felt at ease when the arsonist ended up behind bars.

It was assumed tonight's fire out at Talbot Lake would be no different. He would focus on all possible accidental causes at the beginning, and in this case in particular, he was sure the proper cause would be found right away, a report would be written, and that would be the end. The investigation itself was of little concern though. His issue would be the chief. Jake's nerves were on edge and he was unsure of how to act. How does one console a man who had devoted his life to fighting the very thing that just killed his son?

"Sarah? Hey this is Jake. I hate to wake you, but I need a favor." It was all Jake could do to keep the vehicle on the road as he talked. "Chief Taylor's son just died in a cabin fire over at Talbot Lake and… Yeah I know, it's beyond belief. Listen, what I need is for you to go over there if possible. I'm headed there now and can handle the investigation, but I need you there to head off any conflict of interest… Yeah, okay I'll see you in about forty-five. Thanks Sarah."

Sarah Avery was a fire investigator from the neighboring Johnson County. Jake had worked with her before and thought she would be a good choice for this job. She wouldn't get in the way, and any talk of favoritism would be put to rest if an outside investigator attached their name to the report. Along with a professional relationship, Sarah and Jake had a romantic history together. They had dated briefly but neither was ready for a permanent partner in their lives. Jake was an attractive guy, and he always turned the ladies' heads. He had all the physical attributes - an almond complexion and non-obtrusively muscled body, but what made the women fall for Jake more than anything was his personality. He had a witty sense of humor that could make any situation fun and light-hearted, that paired well with a caring disposition towards everyone he met. Despite all of his great qualities, however, Jake had been unlucky in love. There had been no shortage of women in his life, but finding his soul mate was not yet in the cards.

Jake was handsome, but Sarah's beauty was extraordinary. She had shoulder-length blond hair, finely chiseled looks and stayed in shape with frequent morning runs. Although her outward appearance was noticed by all, her inner beauty is what attracted Jake. Sarah's life was full of heartache. Her mom died at a young age so she had to help her father raise two siblings. Her father was a police officer and his influence led her into the public safety field. She began her career at the Johnson County Fire Department as soon as the age requirement was met, and her ambition stood out to the administration, which led to her rising quickly through the ranks - eventually landing in the arson division.

Watching Sarah work always impressed Jake. Her focus and determination never wavered, and whenever she testified in court, he would try to find an excuse to sit in. He would say the case interested him, or he was studying the defense attorney's line of questioning for future cases. The truth was, he found himself in awe of her demeanor on the stand. He had never seen someone more poised and prepared. She had a talent of taking the most technical aspects of an investigation and turning them into an educational conversation with the jury. After the first few questions Sarah would have them mesmerized with her knowledge and grace, and more than likely the defense attorney would pick up on their admiration of her. It was not unusual for the opposing council to lessen the severity of her cross-examination so they would not alienate the jurors and turn them against the defendant.

Despite their continued friendship, Jake and Sarah had not spoken in a few months. The last time they had seen each other was at a yearly out of town conference, but Sarah was the first person Jake thought of to call tonight. Her experience would be invaluable and having someone to bounce ideas off of was always helpful. Later, however, he would realize that the emotional support Sarah would bring would be more important to him than anything else.

None of this was on Jake's mind as he rushed to the scene, however. All he thought about was coming up with a plan. A simple plan that would include getting in, getting the job done and getting out, causing the chief as little extra grief as possible.

Demon Fire

As Jake drove up the long driveway to the Talbot Lake cabin, he saw the red flashing lights ahead. Turning his own lights off, he pulled as far to the side of the scene as possible. Exiting the vehicle he instinctively took in the surroundings. Jake could tell that his fellow firefighters had done an amazing job of extinguishment. Several engine crews were there, and it looked like they had overcome the problem of not having hydrants around by using the lake to pull water into the trucks and then out through the hoses. The crews now worked on overhaul operations which included making sure all hot spots were out and trying to keep any further damage from occurring. Light smoke and steam emanated from the upstairs windows, and the roof contained noticeable holes cut for ventilation, but the structure was still standing. Jake decided to wait on Sarah so they could delve into the investigation together. While he waited, Jake took initial statements from the on-scene firefighters about what they saw upon arrival and to get first-hand details about the fire.

This was not an easy job. Everyone had known Cole since the day he was born. Growing up around the station is a big part of being the child of a firefighter. From the moment of birth the youngster has a department full of extended family members looking after and caring for them as if they were their own, and this was no different with Cole. As a baby, he was not home from the hospital more than two days when he was taken to the station for the obligatory first photo in front of the fire truck - and of course the weeks before Halloween were spent searching for the perfect infant fire gear to wear.

The responders on scene at the cabin could barely talk about the events of that night. They knew the importance of finding out what happened though, so for the next several minutes Jake pieced together the details of the incident from the various perspectives. Upon arrival of the first engine crew, heavy smoke and flames had vented from the upstairs of the cabin. Chief Taylor could be seen on the porch with Cole as they approached. Each firefighter choked up at this point of the narrative. The Chief was performing CPR. Amazingly his training had taken over, and as he was trying to save his boy orders were called out to his guys such as— "Bring the medical kit; Obtain an arrival time from the ambulance and give them a report; Advise the incoming units that no one remained inside and that the fire attack would will be secondary to the patient." Although the Chief stayed focused on the scene everyone, including Jake was certain that the gravity of the situation would sink in at the hospital.

After the ambulance left with Cole and Chief Taylor, the firefighters turned their attention to extinguishment. The fire seemed to have dissipated while they focused on Cole which was unusual since there were no external forces present that would have caused it to weaken. A fire needs three things to live; heat, fuel and oxygen. The flames furnished the needed heat. The contents and building materials of the cabin provided plenty of fuel and the air itself was adequate to sustain the needed oxygen. For some unknown reason, however, the fire lost strength after emergency crews arrived. Each firefighter noticed the same phenomenon. Jake made a note of these findings and determined that he would find the answers once he got inside for a look.

As he wrapped up the initial interviews, a vehicle pulled up and Sarah stepped out with her camera and notepad in hand.

"Hey Sarah."

"Hi Jake."

The two embraced, and Jake slumped into her arms. He had often worried how he would react to an investigation of this magnitude after someone close had perished, but with Sarah he now realized that with a friend to help, he would get through it.

"It's okay Jake. I'm here for you."

"Thanks Sarah, I guess we should get started."

After the embrace the two approached the cabin as Sarah began to take pictures and log them down. Investigator mode took over, and they both regained focus.

Nothing unusual was noted on the outside. The only fresh tracks on the ground came from either the emergency apparatus or the chief's vehicle, and no sign of forced entry presented itself. The power had been cut by the electric company per the fire department's request, but it was on at the time of ignition. The scene was now lit from external lights that the crews had set up both inside and out. From a cursory glance around the exterior, Jake and Sarah concluded that the fire began inside the structure. It also looked like it might have started on the second floor because the damage to that area looked to be the most extensive. The two investigators walked through the front door which showed little damage other than a small amount of smoke residue. As expected upon entry, they were enveloped by the pungent smell of burned wood and petroleum products.

The first floor of the cabin had a good amount of smoke damage with every square inch seemingly covered in soot. There was little damage from the actual fire though, and charring of the wood and melting of plastics was not prevalent. This led to the assumption by both investigators that most of the destruction would be found on the second floor. After a thorough examination and documentation of the lower floor Jake and Sarah moved upstairs.

Once at the top of the stairs both investigators came to a stop. The majority of the fire had come from an open door leading to what they both assumed was the bedroom.

Demon Fire

This was not strange, but what was unusual was the damage to the flooring just outside the opening. The carpet had a circular area of black soot in the middle of the hallway. The ceiling above this spot was well burned, but there was no noticeable progression from the ceiling to the floor.

Unless acted upon by outside forces, fire moves up and out progressing in predictable patterns. After extinguishment, the progression can be mapped by a visual inspection of the burned areas. There is normally a single ignition source and the fire spreads from that area. If the burned material cannot be traced back to the original source, then a secondary ignition is usually the cause.

"What do you make of that?" asked Jake.

"Well, that is definitely strange." Sarah answered. "How did the fire get from up there to down here? Do you think there might have been some sort of flammable liquid on the carpet? Or maybe it was caused by air flow from the bedroom pushing the fire down."

"Maybe." Jake said. "But that doesn't make much sense. We can take a sample of the carpet to the lab, and maybe they can give us a clue as to what caused this."

"I agree. And the Chief might shed some light on it - if he's not too distraught to remember anything that is. Lord knows I couldn't deal with any of this if it happened to me."

As they walked into the bedroom, a cursory glance around showed that the fire did not originate there. There was extensive damage, but the fire obviously came from the attached bathroom. This was determined by a pattern in the shape of a V that formed from a hole in the wall approximately three feet above the floor. Since fire grows up and out, a V pattern indicates where a fire began with the lower part pointing to a possible origin. In this case, the fire must have exited the hole from inside the wall or from another room. The only problem with this scenario, however, was that there was no flammable material around the hole. The sheetrock had a fire rating of thirty minutes yet the fire pattern showed the wall was burning right from the start.

"Do you see that Sarah?"

"Yeah. There's something about this fire I can't get my mind around."

After photographing the bedroom, Jake and Sarah entered the bathroom which had reached the flashover stage in which all contents ignite. Every item in the room had burned, and it was obvious the origin of the fire was here. A room that has completely burned poses certain challenges to an investigator. The clues that normally show the progression of a fire are found in the backdrop of unburned material. When the entire area is destroyed, the patterns can be hidden.

"We'll have to go through all of the sources of heat in this room to find what caused this one." Jake said.

"I think you are right. I can't imagine the chief lit candles in here, being the fire safety guru he is." Added

Sarah. "There are a couple of power outlets over there that we can look at. I see nothing else that jumps out at me, but maybe something will turn up after sifting through this mess."

"Hey Sarah look over here." Jake pointed to an area beside the sink. "This is the hole that leads to the bedroom." He bent down and looked through to the next room. "Yep. This must be how the fire got to Cole." He stated. "But how?"

Sarah could tell where he was going with the question. The theory of the fire moving from one room to the other made no more sense than the hallway carpet. Although it did in-fact move through the hole, it was not clear how that occurred. The space between rooms was four to five inches, and with fire-resistant sheetrock walls, the fire should not have been able to transfer easily from one area to the other.

"The flames should have entered and burned up through the wall space." Jake noted. "This looks like they were pushed through to the bedroom."

Sarah agreed. "It's like something was forcing the fire somehow."

"Crazy." Jake said with a huff. "None of this is making any sense. Maybe Chief Taylor can shed some light on things."

"Do you need me to finish up here so you can go to the hospital?" Sarah offered.

"I think that's probably the best thing to do. I'm not looking forward to it though. That man has meant the world to me over the last several years, and Cole was like a son to the entire department."

For a brief moment Sarah thought Jake might actually tear up. She had never known him to be an outwardly emotional person. He was always a rock, always the strong one, and he was the one that everyone turned to for support. These qualities are what initially endeared him to Sarah. The romantic feelings between the two never materialized, but seeing his vulnerability peeking through touched something in her she might have explained away at any other point in her life, but tonight was different. Maybe it was being awakened in the middle of the night. Maybe it was the emotions of dealing with the death of someone she knew. She didn't fully understand, but at this point she didn't care about analyzing her feelings. She just wanted to do what she could to help Jake with the investigation and whatever else he might need.

Jake struggled to find a parking space at Trinity Medical Center. After the second trip around the perimeter he was able to squeeze in between an ambulance and a fire engine parked on the side of the road. The hospital was normally busy with ambulances flowing in and out and patients arriving in personal vehicles at all hours of the day and night. The normal traffic situation at the facility was hectic, but the issue was exacerbated by the amount of law enforcement, EMS and fire personnel who had arrived to support Chief Taylor.

Word spreads fast around the public safety community when a tragedy occurs within the ranks. The death of Cole, especially the tragic way in which it occurred, had begun a rapid process of notification throughout the region. Phone calls had been made, social media posts were written and friends and family had arrived.

At the emergency department triage area Jake showed his credentials and was escorted to a private waiting room. He spotted the chief surrounded by several people including Kevin Halburt, the Assistant Fire Chief for the department, and Holland Elster who was the Sheriff for Deer Creek. All eyes turned toward Jake as he approached. He could tell at first glance that along with the emotional pain, Chief Taylor would have to deal with some physical pain from the fire as well. He was wearing a half buttoned shirt with heavy bandaging underneath apparently covering a burned portion of skin.

"Have a seat Jake." It was Chief Taylor speaking with a voice that was hoarse and shaky, but the shocked look on his face was what Jake keyed in on. The full force of what happened had not sunk in yet, and Jake knew his job here would be easier because of it. While the chief was still in shock and denial, he would at least be helpful with the information he gave. When he finally gave into his grief, he would not be able to answer even the simplest of questions. Jake planned on finishing before that occurred.

"Hey chief." Jake did not have much of an idea on how to approach this conversation. He had interviewed dozens of families soon after a loved one had been lost, and he was always thorough and professional. It is always better to interview witnesses promptly, so speaking with the grief stricken was nothing new for Jake, but this was different. Luckily Chief Taylor was helpful in this endeavor.

"I'm glad you're here." The Chief spoke as Jake took a seat. "You don't have to worry with the pleasantries. I know you care for me and Cole. There is nothing that anyone can say to make this better. So let's not worry about that and focus on finding out what happened." Jake knew that the best coping mechanism available was to keep someone's mind focused on a task. This worked well on emergency scenes when a family member was freaking out. The crew would give that person a menial task to focus on such as flagging down the ambulance or gathering home medications. The sense of purpose would coincide with getting their mind off of things which would lead to that person staying out of the emergency workers way. The chief had obviously set his own mind to the task of finding out what happened with the fire. For now, this helped to block out emotions that threatened to overpower him.

The job of Fire Chief is akin to being the CEO of a business. There are hundreds of jobs and tasks that a fire department is expected to accomplish. From fighting residential and commercial fires to confined space rescues, medical calls, vehicle extrications, hazardous materials and of course investigations, there are many specialties firefighters can focus on. Like the aforementioned CEO, a chief is not capable of being an expert in each discipline. The fire engine operator should know more than the chief about water flow and friction loss through a hose. A rope rescue team should know more about high angle rappelling, and an investigator should be more experienced with finding the cause and origin of fires. The chief should, however, have a general knowledge of all of these things, and be able to speak about them proficiently. Chief Taylor had a good understanding about the investigatory process and he went straight into giving as much information to Jake as he might need.

"I stayed up late watching a movie and fell asleep on the couch. Cole's scream woke me, and I jumped up and had to gain my composure because I didn't know where I was right away. Once my head cleared and everything came together, I realized that I was in the cabin and Cole was in his room. He was screaming, so I raced upstairs and smelled something burning as I reached the top. I was scared to death Jake. I saw the smoke coming from Cole's room. It was seeping out from around the edges of the door, and I was terrified of what would be found on the other side, but I couldn't hesitate. I had to get to him one way or the other. At least I was able to think rationally enough to get low before going in."

The chief hesitated at this point. The narrative flowed effortlessly from his lips as he painted the picture of what happened earlier that night, but Jake knew what lay on the other side of the bedroom door. The interview had reached the point where one of two things would happen. Their conversation would continue, and Jake would get the information he needed to piece everything together. Or Chief Taylor would break down and the interview would end.

"Take your time chief. I know this is difficult." Jake said trying to give what little comfort he could.

After a couple of deep breaths were taken and a tear was wiped away Chief Taylor continued. "I was low to the floor. I reached up, opened the door as smoke billowed out into the hallway. Just inside lay Cole motionless. His body was limp as I pulled him into the hallway." At this point the chief reached for a box of tissues and began blotting his eyes as he spoke. Several others within earshot were trying to hold back their emotions, but with little success. "I knew he had taken in a good bit of smoke, but he was not burned so I felt like there might be a chance. My training must have taken over at that point, and I'm thankful it did because if I had frozen up and not tried to save him then I wouldn't be able to live with myself. My focus was sharp though, and I pulled him into the hallway. But, as I was picking him up to take him downstairs, the strangest thing happened." Chief Taylor paused, and several seconds ticked by without a sound.

"What happened?" prompted Jake.

After another few moments he continued. "Well I could see the fire was consuming the bedroom, and there was thick black smoke and flames billowing out from the top of the door into the hallway, but as I reached down to Cole, the fire started falling."

This seemed like an odd statement to Jake. He couldn't remember a time he had ever heard someone describe fire that way.

"What do you mean by falling?" Jake questioned.

"It just fell. Straight from the ceiling, fast like something was pushing it down. I have never seen anything like it before. A cylinder of flames headed right for us. I grabbed Cole and moved toward the stairs, but as I turned, the fire came down with a rush all the way to the carpet. The flames got me, and I felt the pain shoot down the back of my arm and shoulder, but I wasn't deterred. I ran downstairs and took Cole to the front porch. I'm thankful that I had enough sense to grab my cell phone, so I was able to begin chest compressions with one hand and call 911 with the other. I thought it would take the guys forever to get there since we were so far out, but it seemed like a fast response. As I heard the sirens, I felt a sense of relief. I was thinking the entire time that we could save him. Everyone worked so hard Jake. Our guys, the nurses and doctors at the hospital. They all did the best they could. He just took too much smoke and heat into his lungs. There was just no way to get him back."

Violent sobbing followed the narrative. Jake was impressed that the story was able to be told at all, and after a long pause he began to speak a few words that would end the interview. All the needed information had been gathered, and it was time to let the man grieve. Before Jake was able to back away, however, Chief Taylor cleared his throat and asked a question of his own.

"Do you know what started the fire?"

"Not yet. I have Sarah Avery working the scene now. It started in the bathroom, but we don't have a point of origin yet."

"I'm glad she is helping you. I know this has got to be tough for you to deal with, but she will help you get through it." Chief Taylor had always been a fan of Sarah's. He would have loved to have been able to hire her, but she was too loyal to ever leave Johnson County. The Chief also would love to have seen Jake and Sarah stay together. He thought they were a perfect couple, and he never understood why they broke up.

"It is tough." Jake said. "But I know you want answers, and I'll get them for you."

"Thanks Jake. I appreciate that. So it began in the bathroom? There was nothing in there unusual that I can think of. Cole got a shower, but we didn't have any candles and we had nothing plugged in. Did you find anything while you were there?

"No. Not a thing so far. I didn't see any heat sources other than the power outlets. I was hoping you might be able to help us with that."

"I'm afraid I can't. Nothing comes to mind as to what could have started it. I don't have any lighters Cole could have gotten. I just don't know. What is your next step?"

"Well the only thing I can think of is the electrical wires and the power outlets. I will probably get Shane Tandy to come take a look."

"That's not a bad idea. He will give you some definitive answers about that."

Shane worked for the State Arson Division. Because his specialty was electrical engineering, Jake would use him from time to time when certain fires seemed to have been caused by electrical means. He would call him the next day, and with the circumstances of this fire he was sure an answer would be available soon.

"There was one other item I wanted to ask you about chief. Maybe your experience will help out."

"What is it?"

"Well, the fire seems to have moved from the bathroom to the bedroom through a hole about three feet above the floor next to the sink. The opening is about the size of a softball, and there was another hole the same size on the other side. There was nothing flammable around either one so I don't see how the fire could have spread so easily unless some kind of air flow was pushing it, but that doesn't seem plausible, and even if the change in pressure of the rooms was in play, it wouldn't pull enough flame in to spread the fire with only a sheetrock wall as fuel."

"That doesn't make much sense to me. Are you sure the door to the bathroom wasn't open, or maybe it spread another way?"

"No. It definitely went through that hole because of the burn patterns in the bedroom. This fire just didn't seem to act normal." Jake said.

"Yeah that and the fire in the hallway add up to a strange event. Now that you mention it, I remember something else unusual." Before he spoke again, the chief looked off in the distance like he was trying to clear his thoughts. "Well, Cole's scream woke me up. He was upstairs with the door closed, but that scream was so loud and clear I know it will stick with me the rest of my life. As I got up from the couch though, I heard another scream." The chief hesitated again. "I'm not even sure if scream is the right word. It was a strange noise though coming from upstairs as well. I know you and I have both heard many unusual sounds on fire scenes, but this didn't sound like anything I have come across before. It was a horrible noise, but I had forgotten all about it until now. Not sure if that's helpful to you or not, but I just remembered it."

"Chief, you know better than most that any small piece of information can be useful. I'm not sure what it could have been, but I'll definitely make a note of it. I'm sure as the investigation progresses all these questions will be answered."

"Well, I know you can figure it all out. I am glad you are on the case. I'm just sorry that you have to be. Tell me one thing though. The smoke detectors didn't have batteries did they? I didn't realize it but thinking back I don't remember hearing them." Chief Taylor was a little anxious about asking this question because he assumed what the answer would be. At his house, as with any good firefighter, he made sure the smoke detectors were always in working order. The batteries got replaced twice a year to coincide with the time change, and he had spent many years teaching the public the importance of this routine. But the cabin was not his house and the proper operation of the detectors was not something he had considered.

"No they didn't." Answered Jake. "None of the detectors we checked were working."

The Chief's head dropped. The tragedy of the night was overwhelming, but the thought of his child dying from something so preventable was almost too much to bear. Jake placed his hand on the chief's uninjured shoulder. He had placed the chief on a pedestal many years ago. To Jake he was a mentor, a teacher and a hero. To see him have to go through this was tragic, and the only solace he had was the fact that he would not have to ask for any more details about the fire tonight. There would be further discussions at a later date if more questions arose, but for now he had gained all the information needed.

Jake offered a few words of comfort and left the chief in the care of the department chaplain who had shown up a few minutes earlier. The county's coroner had arrived as well, and after a brief conversation, Jake agreed to let him handle the coordination with the crime lab. Cole's body would be transported that night, and Jake had been assured that the technicians would make this investigation a priority. With fatality fires an autopsy is normal procedure to determine the cause of death. A thorough investigator would never leave an opening for anyone to come back at a later date and question how an individual died so even though everyone knew Cole had breathed in too much heat and smoke, a full determination of that would be documented by an outside source. Chief Taylor did not like the idea of his son being poked and prodded on a cold metallic examination table, but he knew it was a necessary part of the process so he made no objections.

Jake spoke to a few of the well-wishers as he was leaving. The same promises of support for his investigation and wishes for a better tomorrow were spoken by everyone there. He knew the chief would be well taken care of that night. The crowd would stay until Cole was transported, and several would offer the use of their homes so he would not be alone. Knowing his boss, however, Jake assumed that he would just go home, sit in the recliner and stare at the TV until exhaustion finally took over.

Back at the cabin Jake found Sarah with notepad in hand finishing a sketch of the area. A good drawing is a valuable reference tool to have when trying to describe a scene to a jury. Dimensions can be documented and notable objects marked while the area is still intact so one's memory would not have to be the determining factor when describing details later.

As Jake approached, Sarah put down the notepad and reached for an embrace. They stood in each other's arms while she whispered a caring word or two in his ear. She knew his meeting with the chief must have been heartbreaking. To Jake the hug, while unexpected, was a welcome respite from the stress. The pain he felt did not compare to the anguish others dealing with this situation faced, but it was difficult, and having someone there who cared about him was more than he could have hoped for.

As the embrace ended he thanked Sarah again for being there for him.

"It's okay Jake. I'm glad I can help. I only wish there was more that could be done. The documentation is complete, and the guys helped me with the initial clean out the fire rooms. We sifted the debris, but still didn't come up with a cause. The power outlets do show signs of internal damage though so it might be a good idea to get someone to look at the electrical system. I would suggest Shane Tandy."

"Great minds think alike. I planned on calling him first thing in the morning. Until then we can wrap things up here for the night. I am still confused about how the fire acted once it got going, but if we can pinpoint where it began we will at least be a little further along."

"Agreed." Sarah said. "Another crew is on the way to relieve these guys. They will rotate out until you release the scene."

"Hopefully Shane will come tomorrow, and I will release it after that. I am looking forward to getting this investigation behind me." Jake lamented.

"I know you are. Go home and rest. You have to take care of yourself during the next few days."

"I will." Jake promised.

"Good. And can you do one more thing for me? This sounds dumb, but will you text me when you get home? I want to make sure you arrive safely."

Jake nodded his approval, and the two parted ways with another long hug. On the way home it would have been normal to be consumed with the tragic events of the night. He began the evening believing his thoughts would be preoccupied with the investigation as well as the concern for Chief Taylor and the rest of the department. He assumed that several sleepless nights of worry and stress lay ahead, but those thoughts were pushed aside at the moment. Right now he could not seem to get Sarah out of his mind. He wasn't sure what might have changed, but he could sense old familiar feelings creeping up inside of him again. Maybe the emotions of the night clouded his judgment, but that did not concern him. He was just happy that his mind could wander to a more pleasant place. He was wandering to those places as he settled into bed, read the response from his text to Sarah and fell sound asleep.

Chris Cumbie

Chapter 3

Reflections

Chris Cumbie

Demon Fire

The sun peeked through the blinds of the living room as the salesman explained to the television audience how much dirt the newest greatest vacuum could handle. While the commercial played, Chief Taylor slowly lifted his right eyelid. The noise emanating from the speakers was excruciating, and the light blinding. The headache he awoke with caused more pain than any experienced before. When he arrived home from the hospital he had cracked open a beer, sat down in the recliner, turned on the television and passed out. He glanced over at the opened bottle next to him and determined that no more than two swallows had been taken. He assumed the exhaustion got to him, but he didn't know how sleep could have been possible with all the built up stress from the night's events. His gaze moved from the beer to the clock. The day would be busy with phone calls to friends and family, and a 9:00 AM start did not sound bad with all things considered.

One call would be to his ex-wife Janet. She arrived at the hospital after Jake left and was inconsolable, but Chief Taylor had been grateful that she laid none of the blame at his feet. She knew their son encompassed his entire world, and he did everything in his power to save him. The notifications to her side of the family would be taken care of, and most of his close family and friends had been contacted early on, but there would be a few members of his extended orbit that would need to hear from him today. After that a call to the funeral home, and then he would touch base with Jake at some point. Maybe later he would visit the fire station to check in on the guys.

He tried to concentrate on everything that needed to be accomplished that day, but the headache was too much to take. The only silver lining was the fact that because of the severe pain, the thought of Cole did not overwhelm him. Stumbling to the kitchen he poured a glass of juice and swallowed enough ibuprofen and acetaminophen to cause his liver and kidneys to wake up and take notice. As he made his way back to the living room, he checked himself in the hallway mirror. He looked like one might expect for the situation, but not bad enough that a shower and a change of clothes couldn't help. Turning toward his trusty seat, he stopped dead in his tracks. A glimmer appeared out of the corner of his eye and looking back into the mirror an extreme sense of déjà vu and vertigo engulfed him. All of the familiarity he once had with the world was gone as he was not seeing, feeling, tasting or comprehending the same way as he had just moments before. The chief's knees buckled, and he almost fell, but managed to steady himself and make it back to the chair without further incident.

He decided that the best course of action was to close his eyes and relax. This feeling had to pass at some point and maybe the medicine would kick in, and the headache would ease. The increased pain and confusion must have been a result of the glare from the mirror, but the more he sat and thought about it, the stranger the situation seemed. He tried to replay in his mind what had just happened. He remembered looking into the mirror the first time and noticing his disheveled self. The glimmer appeared as he turned, but what he saw after that was indescribable.

Visualizing the world through the same eyes, with the same colors, the same shading, the same contrast and from the same vantage point is a constant in most people's lives. That constant changed in an instant for Chief Taylor. It felt like he was looking at his face from two different vantage points. The first view was the one that was familiar to him. It was a simple view of his face. The face he'd known for a lifetime. The face had changed over the years, but those changes were always subtle enough not to cause alarm. The second view had caused the issue. This view had also come from Chief Taylor's eyes yet the image seemed to skew at a different angle. The facial features blurred, and the colors looked as though they were being viewed through a filter. What amazed him as the event was recreated in his head was that both of the views occurred at the same time. This had to have been where the déjà vu and vertigo came from.

    The fear and uncertainty of what had happened should have been enough to keep him from moving for a while, but curiosity got in the way. Slowly, so as not to bring on the unwanted symptoms again, Chief Taylor rose from the recliner and made his way back to the hallway. He had to look in the mirror again. He knew he was not going crazy, but he had to try to put together what just happened. It was assumed that the stress played a role in his issues, but he needed to be sure. When he approached the mirror again his eyes lifted upward, and as his gaze fell onto the face once more, he was relieved that it was once more just his face. Nothing strange. No déjà vu, no vertigo. The same face he had always known was staring back at him.

    A huge sigh released from the depths of his lungs, and he felt better about the situation. Just then another realization occurred. Although it had only been a few minutes, not enough time for any of the medication to work, the headache which was unbearable only a few moments prior had dissipated.

Demon Fire

The sudden madness was almost too much to bear. With the nothingness there had always been self-consciousness. The body had left a long time ago, but the soul survived, and along with the soul, the mind was still intact. The thought processes, the memories and the reasoning skills all remained just as before.

This was an entirely different experience, however. Traversing through fire was akin to riding a wave as the bodiless soul glided from one place to another. The sudden effect of occupying the same space as someone else had not been expected though. Two minds were trying to mesh into one and looking through another's eyes and hearing through another's ears was disturbing. The experience was strange enough, but what made it surreal was that the information transmitted through the senses doubled. Each bit of data entering the shared brain was translated and perceived through two separate minds at the same time. The sensory overload so overwhelmed David that he was inclined to run back into the burning bedroom and once more transition into the flames. This thought lingered only a few seconds before the promise of freedom brought his decision-making process full circle. He would not waste this opportunity. There was no way to know how his plan would unfold once the cabin was vacated. The world outside was as unknown as the body he now shared, but he was already experiencing a change from the normal routine of nothingness and boredom he had experienced for all of those years, and even though the change for the moment had been excruciating, the chance to leave, to experience new things and most importantly the chance to avenge were enough to steel his mind.

    The shared being had not been aware of his presence. All focus remained on the boy, and that was advantageous. Keeping his host unaware would be the first step, and it would be crucial. Having someone fighting against him from the inside would not be beneficial to what he had hoped to accomplish. The second step would be to simply observe and learn about this new world and how to control the unusual environment he was now in. So while the host busied himself with what looked like a strange death ritual composed of pushing on the chest interchanged with periodic blowing into the mouth, David moved back into the depths of the consciousness. It was not a fluid motion though. Unfamiliarity with his situation had caused issues, but he tried to block out the confusion and focus on a safe place to hide deep inside his host, and as the newly formed couple entered a strange carriage with flashing lights, David was able to settle in and begin his observations.

    The world came into focus with a better clarity after a few minutes of practice. The trick was to subdue his interpretation of incoming stimuli and rely instead on the host's understanding. At first it seemed like he was looking at everything through two sets of eyes, but as they entered the largest most brilliant structure David had ever seen, the senses lessened to the point where he could sit back, watch and wait.

The night filled with a myriad of new sights and sounds. Apparently the village now knew of the boy's death, and numerous people arrived to meet with his host. The condolences sounded somewhat familiar although the language had an unusual dialect compared to what he was used to. David spent most of the time watching the interactions between the visitors and his host. Excitement grew about the prospects before him, but enthusiasm was somewhat dampened by the fact that many important questions remained. One question was; how would he be able to control the shared body? At this point total autonomy had been maintained by the host. This was helpful for the moment, but that dynamic would have to change at some point. Dual control was an option, but his first entry into a shared consciousness resulted in an unpleasant experience. Another question turned out to be; how would he find the information needed to implement his plan? David knew the places he searched for existed since almost everyone that night had spoken of them. This society seemed to cling to the same ideals and beliefs during times of hardship and suffering that David had experienced in the past. Knowing of the existence of these places did not translate to knowing their location or having the means to travel to them though, so a good deal of work lay ahead.

As the night grew longer, a realization unfolded. The host had gotten tired, and energy was draining. This slowing down of body and mind felt strange to David. One struggle he had dealt with in the past was the inability to rest. Decades upon decades of being awake had filled his world with no rest at all. The mind was always working, always thinking and always conscious. The torture he had endured in the final passage of life did not compare to the time spent in the nothingness, all alone with no rest to bring peaceful relief.

Although a sense of relaxation was unfamiliar, he remembered it and realized right away that it might be helpful. The body he inhabited would sleep at some point, and David could already tell that controlling the host would be easier in a depressed state. Less concentration was needed to use the senses without the information being doubled. Excitement grew as they left the building, got into a carriage driven by a friend and headed home.

Once settled into a comfortable chair, the host took a couple of sips from a beverage as David prepared himself, and at the moment consciousness retreated he sprang from his hiding place and moved further into the host's mind. There was an immediate reaction from the host, but it was not an issue since David found that it did not take much effort to keep his unwitting partner under control.

David's ease of movement was amazing. Flowing over the billions of neurons was akin to his travels through the waves of flames. He noticed that motion was effortless and he could switch between his and the host's senses with no issues since there was no confusion or doubling of data. David made sure that his first tour included a general overview of the various areas he would need to manipulate. His immediate familiarity with how this new atmosphere operated was impressive. He assumed this was due to the absence of interference from his host's conscious senses, allowing David's gathering of knowledge to proceed unimpeded.

After orienting himself to a basic floor plan of the area David focused on the memory section. Tons of terabytes of data opened to him ready for referencing, but the problem would be filtering the material into useable portions. Priorities dealt with determining location of targets and figuring out how to operate the foreign means of conveyance that this new society relied on. To his delight all of this information was readily available and easily absorbed. His host not only knew the locations of the places David needed, he had been inside most of them. There would be no issues in finding out where he needed to go or what to do once he arrived.

Chris Cumbie

David's orientation proceeded unabated with the next few hours spent delving into the ocean of remembrances. Early memories of childhood birthday parties, teenage crushes and other non-essential items were ignored since he assumed that the recent past would contain the needed guidance. A normal person obtaining knowledge and access to all the changes over the last few centuries might have spent a good portion of time marveling at the wonder of this new world. David, however, was not concerned with any of this. A laser-focused drive pushed him forward with the task at hand, and the only information he was interested in contained facts that would further the progression toward his goal.

Vehicles, cars and trucks were some of the words used to describe the means of transportation they had used to get from the large building, now understood to be a hospital, to his host's home. While not overly complicated, the motor-sensory skills needed to operate such a device would be more than David could master in a short time. There was no worry though since a manned vehicle referred to as a taxi seemed suitable for his purpose and was available whenever needed.

Once the means of transport was determined, David spent the remainder of the evening reviewing language nuances, since the English he had spoken differed from the verbiage of today. Time was also spent studying the immediate area where he was located, as well as other small details such as currency denominations and names of acquaintances. The further into his host's mind he went, the more data he collected. Like a sponge David soaked up every little piece of information needed for the success of his mission.

The hours passed quickly through the night and into the morning with no issues until he realized that something had drastically changed. Fear and uncertainty gripped as an unknown source pulled him away from his memory quest. As he rose back through the depths of his host's mind, he determined that his consciousness was not the only one present. The host had awoken and was doing the worst possible thing imaginable. He was staring into a mirror. The sensory overload that had occurred before paled in comparison with the situation David found himself in now. All the double vision, confusion and fear became magnified. As his host's eyes were fixed to the mirror, it appeared to David as though he was looking at multiple images such as one might do if they held one mirror in front of another.

The effect was excruciating, and he focused all of his energy into retreating to his previous safe hiding place. The host clearly felt the same unease as he stumbled back to the chair, and as David returned to his safe place, his host sat back down. The comfort and calm following the misery, was palpable, and David made a note to never lose focus to the point where he found himself mobile in the mind at the same time his host was conscious again.

Chapter 4
A Colonial Life

Chris Cumbie

Demon Fire

Rachel Devlin's exemplary beauty and charm were juxtaposed against the backdrop of the gloomy environment in which she lived. The settlers of the little community of Haniford Virginia led a hard life, and each day began more or less the same for most of the people who lived there. The women rose before dawn to prepare for the first meal of the day. Then it was on to the laundry which was washed by hand and took up most of their time between cleaning up after the previous meal and beginning the next. The men would wake early, and after eating would proceed to the woods to hunt wild game or travel to the fields to tend the crops. Others would meet up to tackle special projects such as building barns or mending fences. The labor seemed endless for all involved, but there was a hardiness to the society that bonded them together. It was them against the elements, and they had to work hard and stay strong to survive.

Rachel had married at a young age which was not unusual since the quicker a marriage began and children were born the sooner they grew old enough to help with the chores. She and her husband Thomas had begun their family with a boy who filled their quaint little house with love and joy. The couple was well regarded in the community, and although life was difficult, it was a joyous time.

Unfortunately, within a few years after their boy's birth things took a drastic turn for the worse. Thomas farmed for a living, and one day during the spring he had risen earlier than usual. The last frost had passed, and the cornfields had yet to be plowed. A strict schedule was needed for a bountiful harvest so he planned on getting an early start to catch up on his work. Breakfast was foregone since Rachel and his boy would not be up at that time of morning. A quick kiss to the cheek of each while they were sleeping, and out the door he went.

The family horse was a strong determined animal which was advantageous since a good dependable beast was an invaluable asset to a farm. From plowing the fields to hauling timbers, the work productivity increased exponentially with their use. Thomas took great pains to care for his horse, providing him a small barn close to the house with a separate stall always lined with fresh hay and a blanket for warmth during the winter months. Thomas appreciated the importance of his favorite helper, and although it was a hard life for the animal, he tried to make it as comfortable as possible.

The horse was extremely gentle, and he never shied away from his halter or harness. He would even allow Thomas' son to ride on his back during the infrequent downtime around the farm. When he arrived at the barn this day, however, Thomas sensed that something was wrong. The horse seemed agitated. There were several kicks and stomps at the ground followed by loud neighs coming from the horse. This behavior concerned Thomas, and he proceeded with caution into the stall. He knew he was at a distinct disadvantage once inside since the small space and large animal left him little room to maneuver. He assumed something had spooked the animal. Perhaps a snake had entered the area and overacted once it came upon the site of such a large animal. A snake might have bitten the horse or just spooked it, but either way the horse was not happy about his situation or Thomas's presence. If he had not been pressed for time a postponement of the day's activities would have been in order. There were always plenty of other chores to do, but the fields had to be plowed so Thomas pushed onward.

Looking around, he noticed nothing out of the ordinary. If another animal had been at fault for the anxiety, it was no longer present. Thomas ran his hand across the horse's neck as he spoke a few soothing words. There was not a strong reaction although the muscles noticeably tensed. The plowing halter hung by the back wall. Thomas retrieved it and it was placed without incident. A sigh of relief followed, and everything seemed to be okay. Even though his horse was normally even tempered, its sheer size compared to Thomas meant that there could still be a danger in such a tight space. The threat seemed to have dissipated though so Thomas attached the lead rope and opened the gate, but when he gave a tug, the horse's muscles sprang into motion. An ear splitting neigh let out as the horse jerked backwards and raised his front legs. A quick kick forward and Thomas found himself on the ground.

The kick was just a glancing blow, and there were no serious injuries, but a person lying exposed in front of an unsettled animal is not a good position to be in. He did not think there was time to get to his feet, so he flipped over and crawled away as fast as possible. Once outside the stall he would close the gate and figure out from there what his next step would be. Unfortunately he was not fast enough. The horse's legs rose once more and upon landing, a hoof came down on Thomas. The blow was quick, and as soon as it struck the horse became calm once again. The entire incident took no more than ten seconds, but unfortunately that was enough time for serious damage to occur. The blow landed on Thomas' torso, and his ribs gave way to the force. Shards of bone splintered and shot unabated through his chest ripping into the lungs and spleen as blood flowed into his chest cavity, and Thomas lost consciousness.

Rachel woke that morning to find that her husband had left without breakfast. He was prone to leaving early when extra work was to be done or when he got behind so it was not a shock when she found him gone. Her normal routine when this occurred was to proceed with the meal, and then after eating and feeding her son she would take a basket of food out to the field. Sustenance was necessary for a hard day's work, and it was Rachel's job to keep her husband well fed.

Upon arriving at the fields, she looked far and wide. Thomas might be anywhere. The area was expansive, and several men tended to different spots. No one had seen him that morning, and after checking the creek where he would sometimes visit for a cool drink she decided to try and retrace his steps from the morning. She started to become concerned because not much deviation from routine happened in their lives, and a bit of anxiety crept into her mind. The first place she tried after peaking into the house to make sure he hadn't returned there was the barn since Rachel assumed Thomas would have gone there to retrieve the horse. As she entered the shed and saw the animal still in its stall her heart skipped a beat. She knew now that something had to be wrong, and her fear materialized as she peaked over into the stall and saw the limp body of her husband.

Death was not an unusual occurrence for the community, and Rachel was familiar with it. Most diseases and infections had no cures, and the life expectancy of the community was not great so she knew the difference in someone that was unconscious and someone that had passed. Thomas had been down a while, and she could tell he was gone. At that moment of realization it seemed to Rachel that her entire world had been torn apart.

―――――――――――

The day of Rachel's husband's death was fourteen years ago. In the time since, she had adjusted as well as anyone could expect. There had not been a remarriage, which concerned others, but she had been well taken care of by the community. Her main job now consisted of filling in with laundry and cooking chores for families in need. If someone was sick or injured or too old to complete all of their workload, she would help get the work finished. Rachel had lost none of her attractiveness, and most of the community members would argue that she became more beautiful as each year passed.

Demon Fire

Her son had been only four when his father died, and now he was a strong young man who had turned into an asset in the fields. His hands were rough, but his heart was happy. He had reached a good age to begin a family of his own, but he had yet to choose a bride. It had nothing to do with a lack of interest from girls. He was smart, kind and had inherited his mother's stunning looks. It was more of a lack of importance to him. The time spent farming and making sure his mother was well cared for were his priorities, and he was fine with his allotment in life.

In the years that had passed since the tragedy the community had grown. Good weather and a strong work ethic had produced an abundance of food, and the surrounding timber provided materials for new and bigger buildings that dotted the landscape. Families were reproducing, and the population had an additional boost from an influx of migrants. One newcomer to the town was a man by the name of Alden Sinclair. Pastor Sinclair, as he was known, had dazzled everyone upon his entrance into town. He had ridden in on the most spectacular horse anyone had ever seen. At that time, the only familiarity the town's people had with horses were the ones that worked in the fields. They were good sturdy animals, but not what anyone would call impressive. A short stature and mild demeanor was the norm, and most of the farmers stayed too busy to keep them clean or well cared for. A field horse's job dealt with pulling heavy loads and plowing, and not much else was expected of them. The beast that Pastor Sinclair perched himself upon, however, was splendid. Bay colored, proud and tall, and everyone became enamored with both horse and rider. The horse was impressive for its stature and poise, and the rider for his oratory skills and expansive knowledge about biblical and world history.

According to Pastor Sinclair's rendition of his life, he was a well traveled man. From the cities of Europe to the frontier of the Americas, it seemed that he had been to everywhere imaginable. Most people of Haniford would never travel over twenty miles away at any point in their lifetime so listening to stories from someone who had seen and experienced so much was eye opening, and quite pleasurable. To bolster his recollections the pastor would often produce trinkets such as buttons, pottery pieces or aged papers he claimed had significance in some strange foreign place. A few of the tales were outlandish, but the town's people were a trusting group and had no reason to question the validity of the stories.

Pastor Sinclair's arrival did not bring the religious experience to Haniford. As in most places in Colonial America, a centralized building was used for church services. There were few bibles available, but the literacy of the area was lacking so it did not make much of a difference. The few men that could read and understand the sometimes-difficult text took turns speaking to the gathered groups during Sunday meetings. This arrangement seemed to suit the needs of all involved, but with the pastor's appearance six years ago things changed as he took over all of the spiritual responsibilities. No one was opposed to this since he was better versed at the teachings of Christianity than anyone else, and his passion during sermons charged up the congregations. Even the most subdued members could not keep their frenzied excitement contained during his fire and brimstone orations.

Soon after his arrival, the church building doubled in size and had ample living space attached for the pastor's home. Sunday service became a mandatory practice with most of the day set aside for sermons and private counseling sessions - which included individual and family-oriented time with the pastor for more in-depth consulting and one-on-one teaching about the gospel and how it applies to daily life. Along with these new changes, several social events and various meetings were also scheduled at the church. These affairs were enjoyed by all and gave a needed respite to the chores and hardships of normal life, although the social nature always had a strict undertone of religious adherence.

Pastor Sinclair never missed an opportunity to bring his word to the masses, and during his tenure the church became even more entrenched in the daily operations of the town. Religion was not only to be a part of Sunday services, socials and special events - it was to be engrained in society to the point that each decision throughout a person's life would be made after asking the question, "What would God do?" and maybe more importantly, "What would Pastor Sinclair do?"

Religion is a lot of different things to different people. For some, it is a bastion of hope in a world where hope is not always abundant. For others it's the embodiment of love for themselves and all mankind. A belief in a Higher Being gives purpose and sustainability to a sometimes difficult life, and it gives believers an idea that their essence will continue after the toils of this world are complete. For some, however, religion is a tool. It is a means to an end and a way to manipulate people in order to gain power and control.

Pastor Sinclair fell into the latter category. He was well read in the studies of religion. Bible verses could be quoted and applied to almost any situation, and he always knew how to relate the written text to his parishioner's individual lives. He was also well spoken and could talk in a fatherly and professional manner and then seamlessly transition to a more down-to-earth loving and caring tone. These traits made it easy to guide the community much like a puppeteer would lead his marionette.

Demon Fire

This manipulation went unnoticed by the town's people as most were ignorant about life and the world outside their confined area, and there was no one to tell them any different other than the pastor. The outsiders that passed through saw nothing out of the ordinary about the town or its people. The underlying evil that was part of Haniford could not be seen from the surface so the casual observer recognized little that would be concerning. Pastor Sinclair was a master of camouflaging the negative aspects of his life, and he was also a patient man. He pushed the tentacles of his church into the various parts of the community slowly. He would wait until a need arose, then he would make the church available to fill the objective. Examples of needs that were taken over by the church included organizing land distribution, asset allocation, construction schedules, family planning and a myriad of other tasks and services for the people, including running the local schoolhouse.

One item of importance that came under the church's purview dealt with dispute resolution. Few disagreements ever arose, but there was the occasional question of right and wrong that needed to be answered, and Pastor Sinclair was more than willing to decide the various matters, and the disputants were more than willing to let him. To this end, and not wanting an opportunity for advancement of his influence to go unexplored, the pastor did not waste time transitioning from the role of arbitrator to the unquestioned judge of all things right and wrong.

No set of written rules or regulations and no formal laws were available to enforce when the pastor first arrived, but that soon changed under his leadership. He made sure that the parishioners realized that any and all laws came from the Bible, and since he was the interpreter of God's word to the people, the laws inevitably came from him. Most of the new statutes dealt with mundane topics, such as how much time each week should be devoted to attending or working for the church. Rules were passed about how the people were expected to treat one another and laws requiring all children to attend the church school a certain amount of days per year.

Punishments for infractions of the rules varied depending on the perceived severity. A failure to send the appropriate amount of food to fill the church's kitchen each month might get a public admonishment, which in such a tight knit community would be quite the cruel punishment to most of the town's people. A failure to adhere to a child's attendance requirement at school needed a harsher sentence since the children's education, especially in the teachings of the church, were of utmost importance. This infraction might result in a confinement of one or two days in a small shack that sat one hundred yards to the rear of the church. The confinement shack had no comforts, and there were no amenities including no furnishings. A hard dirt floor was the only bed available although a blanket could be brought in for warmth during the cold months. There were few times that the confinement shack had to be used though because most of the people who had to spend time there made it a point not to return. The length of stay in confinement was not exorbitant though since keeping an adult away from his or her duties to the community and the church was not productive. Of course the pastor determined all guilt and punishments in his capacity as judge. For the most part though, everyone was happy with this system.

Although most of the laws were simple, one trumped all others. That law was against heresy, and it held the most importance as far as Pastor Sinclair was concerned. The heresy statute criminalized beliefs and opinions that ran contrary to doctrine. The church was paramount above all, and its teaching would not be questioned. The pastor reigned supreme, but he thought that if his kind of absolute power was ever doubted his grasp could be loosened. Therefore the heresy law was written to stamp out any dissention before it began.

Most laws carried light sentences, but a few, such as murder, could lead to death. Although there had never been a time in which such an extreme punishment was necessary, preparations had been made in case the occasion arose. To this purpose elaborate scaffolding was constructed next to the confinement shack. The gallows sat in plain sight of the church to serve as a reminder of the importance of conformity.

The act of heresy, like murder, was also punishable by death. In fact, death was the only sentence available upon conviction. Pastor Sinclair made it a point that there would be no leniency for the utmost crime, and no lesser sentencing would be an option. If someone opposed the church he or she would inevitably be killed. But for heresy, the gravest of offenses, the gallows would not be used. According to the pastor a person committing such a crime would be burned alive with the flames of retribution acting as a preview for what the heretic would experience for eternity once they arrived through the gates of Hell.

Symbolism held considerable importance for the pastor, and he would go to great lengths to use comparative examples to paint a vivid picture for his parishioners. Fire had a distinct familiarity among the people of that time. Its uses were innumerable, and because it was such a big part of their lives, most understood the possible torment associated with it. This pain was described during church services in detail when comparisons would be made to the teachings of the Bible and how suffering would follow into the afterlife if they traveled the wrong path while living. Few worried though. Everyone did their best to abide by the teachings, and most felt comfortable knowing that if their pastor's lead was followed then they would never have to fear retribution either in this life or the next.

"Calm down son! You have to get a hold of yourself!" exclaimed Cyrus. "You have to slow down and tell me what's wrong!" David Devlin had burst into the small cabin where Cyrus and his wife Susan had lived alone since their youngest son married and moved out.

"I...I don't know what to do Mr. Cyrus. I need help. I need you to help me. My mom she needs..." His words trailed off as a visible shiver passed through him. "Pastor Sinclair he...he was hurting her!"

"Pastor Sinclair is hurting your mom? That's ridiculous!" shouted Susan.

"Susan hush and let him speak! If you want to help go get a cloth for his hand!" Blood trickled down David's hand as a purple hue formed around the knuckles. Susan realized that she had forgotten her place in the hierarchy of this conversation and left for the kitchen, murmuring apologies to her husband.

"Forgive my wife. She was merely startled at your last statement. Now try and think about what you are saying and tell me what is going on."

The Williams' house was not the first one available. David had passed several places on his way there, but Cyrus, being one of the town's elders was well respected by the community and by David. Until Pastor Sinclair had arrived, Cyrus had been the most articulate and well read of anyone, and his advice was still sought out by most. Cyrus did not oppose the changes since the pastor's arrival, but he had made it a point to keep a sense of autonomy even though he attended the obligatory church meetings and contributed his fair share of goods. David felt he would at least listen, and if anyone in the area could help, then Cyrus would be that person.

"My mother and I were at the church for a private counseling." David began. "We were with Pastor Sinclair in his study, and everything seemed fine. He was just talking about the normal stuff he always talks about, and then he asked me to leave and let him speak with her alone. I didn't think anything about it so I went outside. He said it might take a while, so I went for a walk through the woods. After a while I went back to the church." David paused, and as his eyes looked at the ceiling a single tear made its way down his face following the crease of the nose until it came to rest between his lips.

"Continue David. I am listening. There is nothing to fear. Just tell me what happened so I might help." David took his sleeve and wiped the liquid away as a stern resolve crossed his face and he continued.

Demon Fire

"When I went back inside the church, I heard a scream coming from the pastor's house. It sounded like my mom, but that didn't make sense since she and the pastor were in the study when I left. I had to find out because I knew someone needed help. The side entrance was open, so I went inside. I could hear noises coming from the bedroom so I walked to the door. My mom's voice could be heard from the other side screaming – "No!" I knew she was in trouble, but the door was locked so I kicked it in."

David's voice never wavered as he told this portion of the story. He was determined to get the facts out and to get his mother the help she needed. Cyrus sat aghast at the description of the pastor's semi nude body lying on top of Rachel, and at the description of the separate pairs of eyes, each showing a different emotion. The pastor's eyes held an intense rage that David had not seen before while his mother's had a look of fear and despair. There was some confusion on David's part about what he saw because although in the opinion of the community David was old enough to have taken a wife and have children, he had not yet done so. Therefore he had never taken part in anything sexual. There had been mumblings from friends though, and he knew what his own body's capabilities were so there was no question about what the pastor was trying to force upon his mother.

Chris Cumbie

As he entered the room, Rachel continued to plead for help and as she turned toward David he saw blood trickling from her mouth. Upon his mother's plea David became laser focused. All of his confusion and anger at the event unfolding before him boiled up inside, and he barely felt his feet on the wooden floor as the distance was covered between him and the bed. His love and adoration for his mother was unquestioned. She had raised him alone since the age of four, and since that time he never had a need go unfulfilled. She was the most loving and nurturing person he had ever known, and she had brought him up to be a strong determined young man. As David made it across the room, all of that strength and determination came down on the pastor's face in the form of a fist. The rage in the eyes of the pastor gave way to tears as the bone and cartilage in his nose was crushed by David's soon-to-be bruised knuckles. The blow stunned the pastor, and he lost control of his prey as Rachel slipped out from beneath him.

After the initial shock from the hit, Pastor Sinclair quickly regained his bearings and sprang into action leaping in the direction of the knife he kept by the dresser on the far side of the room. In an instant it was in the pastor's hand as he made his way towards where David stood. Rachel tried to keep her ripped clothes together as she attempted to intervene in the dispute, but the pastor shoved her to the floor violently. David hesitated at the door not sure of the best course of action. He decided to run and hoped the pastor would follow, leaving his mother time to escape. The hesitation almost took too long though, and as David turned to make his break the left hand of the pastor brushed his shoulder as it reached for enough shirt to pull him back into the room.

"All I knew to do was run." David added. "I ran as fast as I could down the drive and only looked back once to see my mother running toward the woods on the opposite side of the church. I knew she would be safe long enough for me to get help so I kept going. Mr. Cyrus I didn't know who else to come to. I didn't know who else might believe me."

Cyrus sat silent as David finished. His wife had tried to reenter the room at one point but was sent back to the kitchen with a stern look from her husband while the story continued. Several seconds passed as Cyrus contemplated what he had just heard. He prided himself a considerate man, and when he spoke his words were always meaningful and well thought out.

"David you mentioned that you thought I might believe this story. In retrospect you must have thought that I might not believe it as well - correct?" David's heart sank as hope left his body. He knew speaking out against Pastor Sinclair would not be easy. A young kid like himself telling such a story about a man as important and powerful as the pastor would certainly lead to skepticism. His hope had hinged on Cyrus believing him, but that scenario seemed to be fading.

"I am not necessarily saying I think you are lying, but is there any chance you could have seen things differently than they really occurred?"

David's head sank into his hands as he sobbed. The fear for his mother's safety had not subsided, and now he was not sure what to do next.

"Everything… everything I said is exactly what happened!" David spoke with a hint of anger to his voice.

"Okay. Try to stay calm. I will do what I can to help you, but I'm not sure where to begin. I would normally seek council from the pastor on a matter such as this, but I do not think it would be appropriate in this instance. I assume then that we would need to speak with Constable Matthews. He will listen to what you have to say and then maybe guide us toward our next step. Do you approve David?"

"Yes sir, and I thank you for your help. I didn't know where else to go."

"There is no need for thanks. I have accomplished nothing yet, and I do not promise to in the future. All I can assure is that I will assist you to the best of my abilities."

Chapter 5
Awakenings

Chris Cumbie

Sarah lay awake in bed for an hour after getting home. The night had been both stressful and enlightening. Her feelings conflicted with the pain and suffering she knew everyone felt with the loss of Cole, and with the unexpected emotions about Jake that could not be shaken. She was a little disappointed for feeling this way. She and Jake had dated in the past, but she had prided herself on maintaining control of her emotions. Her focus had always been on her career, health and well-being. She had not let emotions get in the way of her goals and aspirations before, but now she could tell that a fondness might be simmering. Just like a tickle in the back of the throat that turns into a cold, she knew these feelings might progress, and she was determined not to let that happen.

After she awoke the next morning, Sarah began her daily routine. A big part of what made her strong was her adherence to keeping a good regimen. She was out of the bed each day at 5:00 AM. This happened whether she got in bed at a decent hour or not. The coffee maker always had a timer set for her to have a fresh cup waiting so she would take a couple of sips then slip into the shower. The purpose of a shower was not to clean, however. She used it as a tool to help awaken, believing the steam and heat were better than caffeine to charge up her system. After the shower she would put on a set of workout clothes and either spend an hour in her home gym or more than likely, hit one of the various running trails close to the house. After that she would take another shower, this time for cleaning not waking, eat a quick breakfast and she was ready for the day.

Today was no different, and by 6:00 her run was well under way. She had taken one of the Kaleton Hill Trail's more scenic routes, and the steep terrain made for an extreme workout. Sarah had decided that a hard run would help her focus. The investigation was forefront in her mind which conveniently pushed any unwanted thoughts about Jake to the rear. She just couldn't seem to get past all the anomalies that had occurred with the fire, and the way it acted made no sense to her. It was too early to chance waking Jake with a phone call, but she would make it a point to contact him at some point during the day to see if he had anything new to share.

Demon Fire

For now though, she would run. Over the creek, through the ravine and up the hillside she went. Mile after mile ticked off as she progressed with her hair tucked through the back of a baseball cap, sweat glistening off her arms and legs. She ran further and faster than she had in a long while, and by the time the highest summit of the trail was reached, she had decided to bury any feelings that might creep up between her and Jake. Everything would be kept on the same professional level they had maintained since their dating days. Her focus would remain on herself and her career. Finding room in her life for a relationship was not in the cards at the moment, and Sarah was determined not to let a tragic event and the emotions that came with it change her mind.

Jake awoke startled. He was not prone to nightmares, but the sweat soaked pillow was a visible reminder of the one which just occurred. He assumed that the stress of recent events had gotten to him, and as he lay in bed, the previous night's events replayed in his head. His first thoughts focused on Chief Taylor and the pain and agony this morning must entail. Jake wished he would have been able to wrap up the investigation already. A simple cause and origin determination would have been preferable, but no clear answers had revealed themselves, only more questions. It would do no good to worry, however, since it would not help the process along. He was bound and determined to get this thing finished today so he could back away and let everyone grieve in peace.

Like Sarah, Jake had a morning routine. His day began a little more subdued though with the snooze button being one of his best friends. No sleep compared to the few minutes in between snoozes. Most nights he would even set the alarm earlier than normal just to enjoy a few extra precious moments in bed. When he finally would get up, there was no jumping in the shower or going for a run or anything that required effort. He would usually stumble to the kitchen, make a cup of coffee and then head straight to the sofa and veg-out in front of the news while consciousness materialized.

This morning the same routine occurred, and soon after he got out of bed Jake was on the couch sipping a hot beverage and trying to collect his thoughts. All the items on his itinerary that day ran through his mind. It would be a busy one full of phone calls and meetings. The fire scene would eventually get revisited to see if anything new stood out better in the light of day, and he would try to have Shane Tandy and Sarah meet him there. Jake paused in his thoughts for a moment and took in a deep breath. Thinking about Sarah sent a warm feeling throughout his body, and he was more than willing to enjoy the moment. She had definitely stirred up something in him the night before. He assumed that the feelings were due in part to the tragic circumstances they were sharing, but sleep had done nothing to chase away those thoughts.

After a quick shower and shave it was off to the office. While there Jake made all the necessary phone calls. He spoke with the Crime Lab which had advised that the autopsy was proceeding, and the report would be ready soon which meant Cole's case must have been fast-tracked. Jake was not sure who might have sped things along, but he guessed that someone of importance had called in a favor, and he was grateful of that fact. The body would be released shortly, and a proper funeral could take place to hopefully begin the healing process.

Jake also spoke with Shane Tandy and they agreed to meet at the cabin after lunch. Sarah said she would be there also which Jake was thankful for, though he was a little apprehensive. He was nervous about how to act or what to say which perplexed him since he had never been timid around her before. Even before they dated, a comfort level had been established that had never wavered until now. Conversations flowed naturally between the two, and Sarah always seemed interested and attentive to what he was saying. She was well versed in many topics and usually had something interesting to add to whatever they spoke of.

Chris Cumbie

Jake steadied his thoughts and turned his attention to the next item on the list, which was to check on Chief Taylor. No one had heard from him that morning. Several of the guys at the department had tried calling to no avail - not really surprising under the circumstances. Jake assumed that the chief would not want to talk to anyone knowing he would be answering the same questions and listening to the same condolences as he had the night before. People rarely knew what to say to someone who had suffered such a loss. It was not appropriate to ask how someone was doing because they obviously were going through a terrible time. Telling a person that their loved one went to a better place was reliable, but it did little to comfort the fact that they might not want them in a better place at the moment, they might just want them to still be alive. There were really no good conversations to be had, so Jake understood if the chief was avoiding everyone altogether. But, a welfare check was necessary, and he was the one that must do it.

Jake did not visit Chief Taylor's home often, but when he had an excuse to stop by, he had always been envious of the scenery. Jake's home was nice and quaint, and it had enough room and yard for a single man, but the chief's place seemed homier. Woods surrounded the residence on all sides, and the long driveway provided enough distance to avoid the noise of the road. The wooded view along the drive was broken in several places where rolling fields of pasture peaked through, and old barns and buildings could be seen along the way. Jake had fallen in love with the location the first time he had seen it and now a peaceful calm surfaced as he drove through. He had never lived far out of town, but he could picture himself in a place like this - away from the lights and sounds of the city. A place where he might relax after a day at work and cuddle in with someone special to watch a movie by the fireplace. For a split second Jake pictured himself next to that imaginary fireplace with Sarah. He shook his head and tried to focus on the task at hand. No one had seen Chief Taylor since the night before, and although there was not much concern he would do anything harmful, that thought did find its way into the back of Jake's mind.

Jake brought himself back on point as the chief's house came into view. It was a simple little craftsman style with a full front porch and double dormers. The woods were cut back around the house, and the yard was well maintained with decorative trees and bushes surrounding. The yard always stayed nice and neat and the chief took great pride in showing it off to visitors. Jake was feeling good about things as he stepped out of the vehicle. The air was fresh; the sun shown bright, and he thought the day might turn out better than expected. This positive outlook turned dark as he stepped up on the porch though. Nothing out of the ordinary was heard or seen, but an unexplainable thickness hung in the air. Jake's shoulders sunk like a weight had been placed upon them and he feared what he would find inside.

A deep breath was taken in, held for a second and then released as he reached for the doorbell. He paused suddenly with his finger hovering at the button, and Jake thought about backing away and calling for someone to come out there with him. The thought passed quickly since no one was near, and God forbid he waited for backup while the chief might be inside needing help, so with the finger now touching the button Jake took another breath and pushed. The chimes could be heard inside, but no other noises were present. He waited for what seemed like forever before ringing again and then again and then knocking and then banging. Jake was on the verge of panic when he heard movement inside. He knocked again and called out for Chief Taylor.

"Yeah, who is it?" Came a harsh voice that sounded like it could be the chief's, and Jake knew it should be the chief's, but there was something unusual about it.

"It's me Jake. Is that you chief?

"Yes it's me, give me a second." More shuffling around and then a crashing sound followed by locks turning.

"Come in." The chief said as he opened the door and turned back toward the living room. Jake entered and scanned the surroundings. The darkness in the house led to an overpowering sense of dread that seemed to permeate through his bones. Jake sat in a chair off to the side as Chief Taylor slumped into his recliner.

"I feel bad Jake, really bad."

Jake believed him. No one could look as shoddy as he did without feeling comparably lousy. "I can't imagine what you are going through losing Cole like that. I wish there was something I could say or do to make things better."

"It's not that Jake. Believe it or not I haven't even thought of Cole all morning - until you mentioned his name. I swear that should be the only thing on my mind, but I just can't focus on anything. All I have done this morning is sleep, and when I do wake up, I have the worst headache of my life. I seem to be focusing a little better with you here, but I don't know what is wrong with me. I guess it has to be the stress, but this is pretty unnerving."

Jake felt uneasy about being there, and he was concerned with the chief's appearance and actions. "Do you think it might do some good to shower up and maybe eat? I will wait around if you like, and we can go into town and have breakfast at the diner."

"I know you mean well, and getting out of the house would probably be best for me, but I don't have the energy at the moment. I will stay here and rest for a while longer. Maybe I will get out at some point. Maybe stop by and see the guys. What are your plans for the day Jake? Are you going back out to the cabin?"

"That's the plan. Shane Tandy and Sarah are supposed to meet me there this afternoon. I expect to have better answers by the end of the day. I will keep you informed of course."

"I would appreciate that. I think it's about time for a nap now Jake. Thanks for coming over to check on things. My phone will stay on so give me a call if there is any new information."

"I will chief, and you call me if there is anything you need. I can come back over later and bring groceries or a takeout order if you are not up to leaving the house."

"Okay. I might take you up on that offer. You can show yourself out."

As Jake exited, he looked back and saw that Chief Taylor had already closed his eyes against the world. A two minute visit had not been expected. The trip down the driveway took longer than his conversation with the chief, but the welfare check could have ended much worse than it had. Jake was thankful that the chief had at least been home and alive, but the visit didn't make Jake feel any better about the situation.

"Sorry I'm late." Jake said as he entered the upstairs bathroom of the cabin. Shane and Sarah were crouched down examining the electrical wiring they had pulled from the

Demon Fire

walls. "You two have been working up a storm since I've been gone." All of the debris had been cleared away, and Jake was impressed with the thoroughness in making sure no stone had been left unturned.

The two did not move from their crouched position as Shane made a motion for Jake to join them. "Look at this buddy!" Shane had a tendency to get excited when it came to electricity and fires, and he did little to hide his enthusiasm when he was able to share knowledge with others. "Come down here where you can get a closer look."

Jake crouched down, shuffled a few inches closer and leaned in. Even against such a backdrop as this, Sarah looked amazing. If there was any question as to the feelings from the night before, there was none now. He was a little perplexed at her reaction though. Her greeting was kind and included a smile, but nothing much in the way of emotions came through in her voice or body language. That seemed odd based on the signals he had received before, but that had to be of little concern to him at this moment. He had a job to do so his focus turned to the power outlet Shane was holding.

Jake had seen what Shane showed him many times before. There was a burned area on the back of the outlet that could be traced up and out over the cover.

"This is your culprit right here. Whoever installed these did a terrible job. See this connection here?" Shane took the end of a screwdriver and rocked the wires back and forth. "Loose as can be. I've checked all the connections and most are the same way. Someone just got sloppy." There was disdain in his voice as he spoke. "It kills me that something as simple as taking the time to do a task right could have prevented this tragedy. I see it all the time and it really chaps my hide!" One thing Jake liked about Shane was the plain and simple way he talked. He never tried to impress people with his linguistic skills and pretty much said whatever entered his mind.

"That's about what we had figured." Jake said. "I appreciate you coming out though. With the circumstances I would rather have an expert make the call on the electrical side."

"Well that is definitely the call. There were remnants of a curtain found under the debris so that would have been the way it spread once the fire got going. I will trace everything back to the breaker box and write you up a detailed report and that should be it on my end. Before I leave though, Sarah had asked me to look at a couple of areas of concern you guys had. One was this hole right here. She said the fire moved from here to the bedroom this way." Shane pointed to the hole next to the sink as he spoke. "I'm kinda on the same page as you are on this. I don't know what the heck happened. It doesn't make much sense how it could move so forcefully through that little hole into the other room. She also showed me the hallway and the burned area on the carpet. Again I don't have a clue. I've seen some crazy stuff, but nothing like that. It looks like the fire simply came down from the ceiling, and you say the chief and Cole were right there on the floor at the time?"

"Yeah that's what the chief said." Sarah added. "They were right below the fire when it came down on top of them and burned the chief.

"Well shoot, I know I shouldn't make light of the situation, but danged if it doesn't sound like you have some supernatural junk going on here." Shane said as he let out a chuckle. Jake and Sarah laughed as well. The situation was serious, but having a moment of levity made the job a little more bearable. Soon after entering the public safety field one realizes that laughter is a good coping mechanism to abate the horrors that are encountered.

"I guess there needs to be a new category of fire causes." Jake said. "Natural, accidental, incendiary and now other-worldly." Another round of laughter as Jake and Sarah left the room and headed back outside.

"Well, that should about wrap this investigation up." Jake stated. "I should get a call later today about the autopsy, but there will be nothing in it that we do not know already. The strange occurrences might have to go unexplained, but that will not change what started this fire.

"I think you are right." Added Sarah. "I'm glad you can at least put this away and maybe take time and grieve properly yourself."

"I'm glad it is over. The ones that hit close to home are tough. Thank you again for all the help. It really means a lot that you came down when I needed you."

"You know you can call on me anytime. I'm always here to help if needed. Keep me up to date with the arrangement details okay?" Jake agreed, and they parted ways with a hug. This embrace was different from the one the night before since Sarah was bound and determined to maintain the promise that her emotions would be kept in check. A sense of independence was of utmost importance to her, and that was not going to change anytime soon.

Thoughts of Sarah filled Jake's mind on the drive back to the office. He was unsure of why her attitude had changed. Maybe she was building a wall between them again. He remembered the change that took place the last time they had dated. . There was not a gradual winding down of emotions that might be difficult to notice, but more of a sudden change that affected every aspect of their relationship. Jake assumed that she was getting a head start on fortifying her wall now to protect from future heartache. This realization disappointed him, but it did little to diminish the feelings he had building up. There was no wall on his side. There might be a brick or two to step over, but nothing that would keep him from trying to rekindle what they once had.

Jake's office was a medium sized room at the end of a long corridor located in the fire department headquarters. The area held multiple offices for personnel such as inspections, shift commanders and the assistant chief. The closer an office sat to the main lobby the larger the size and the more important the occupant. Jake enjoyed his location since the further down the hall one went, the quieter it became.

Once he settled in behind the desk, Jake began compiling his report. All information had to be organized and narrated in a clear and intelligible manner since a determination of an accidental cause did not negate the fact that a thorough report must be filed. Some investigators dreaded this part of the job, but Jake took pleasure in seeing a story unfold across his computer screen. From summarizing interviews to explaining the fire's progression from beginning to end, Jake could picture the reader becoming more enlightened as the details were absorbed. Although most of the report would never be read by anyone other than him, there were many occasions during civil or criminal cases that what he wrote would end up changing people's lives so Jake took great care in making sure he noted everything accurately.

Chris Cumbie

During breaks from typing, several phone calls were made. One was placed to Sarah thanking her again for the help. She was not cold, but her attitude was not very pleasing either. He then placed a call to the Crime Lab. The autopsy had just finished, and the preliminary findings concluded what Jake had thought from the beginning. Smoke inhalation would be the final determination of death with nothing else of note found. The test results of the carpet samples were also available showing no flammable liquids were present at the location where the chief's burn took place. After that call, Chief Taylor was next. Jake filled him in on what Shane Tandy determined with the outlet as well as what the autopsy results were. The chief seemed groggy and uninterested, but he thanked Jake for the information and promised that he was doing fine and there was no reason for anyone to come over that night. Jake agreed reluctantly to respect his wishes, and after all the phone calls were complete, his focus shifted back to the report. Hours ticked by and before long dusk arrived.

Jake noticed the shadows crossing over his desk and decided he would end work for the day. As he collected his things and walked through the parking lot, he realized that he was the last one to leave. He had worked a little later into the evening than planned, but that was not an issue. There were no big plans on the horizon other than to shower, eat and watch a little TV before bed - so a late night at the office was not a problem. Once home and relaxed he would try to put the events of the last two days out of his head and get some much needed rest which was easier than expected although the one thing he could not remove from his mind that night was Sarah.

Chris Cumbie

Chapter 6
Flash Point

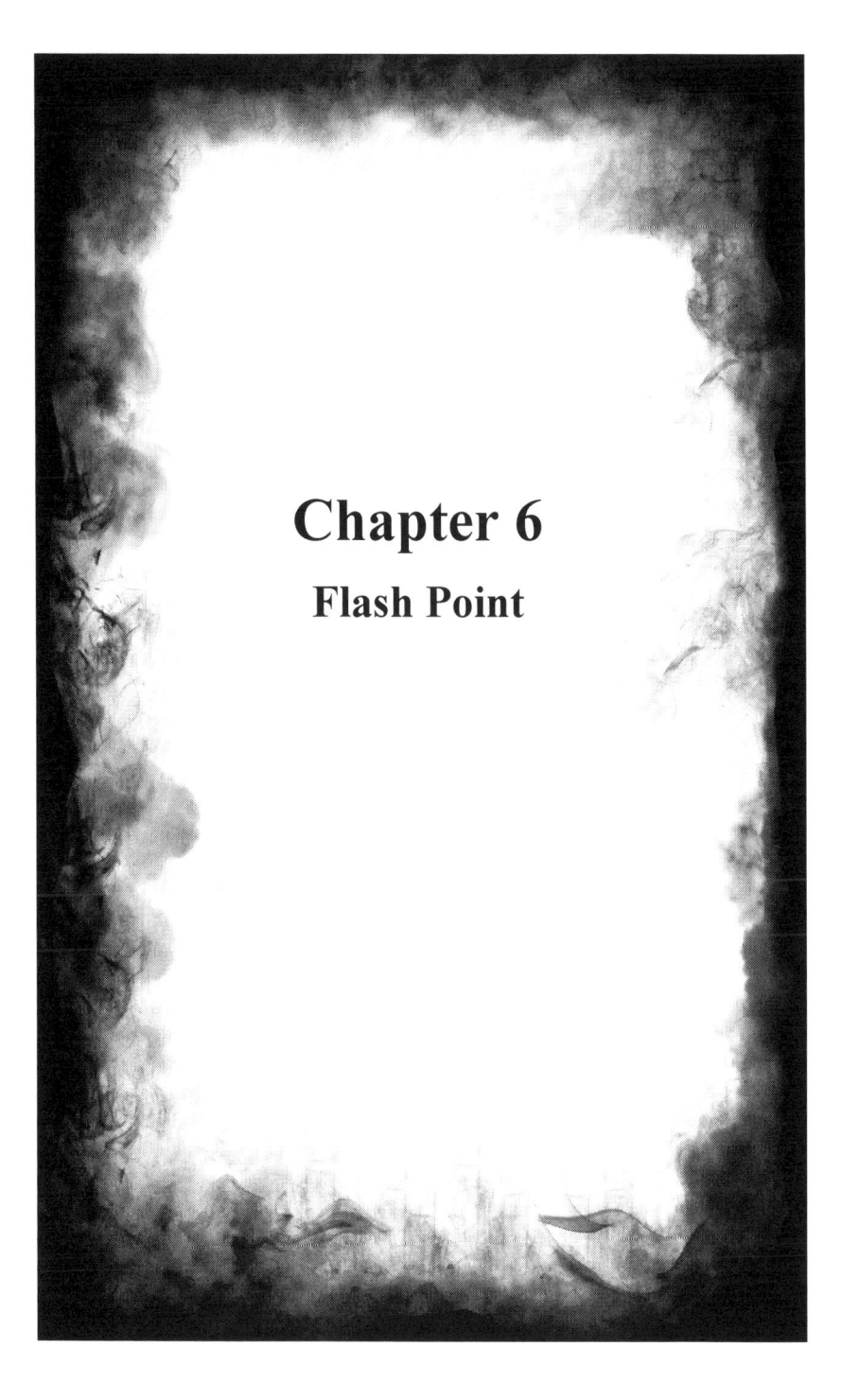

Chris Cumbie

Sarah rolled onto her side and grabbed the cell phone to see who was calling. Only two Jakes had a place in her phone contact list, and one of those had not been heard from in months so that narrowed down the options. She had an idea that this phone call would come, but she wished it had come earlier in the day before laying down for the night. The feelings present the night before were forefront in her mind, and she knew that just because she had made a conscious decision to keep things on a professional level did not mean Jake had.

"Hello."

"Hey Sarah I need you!" Jake said, but Sarah was ready.

"Jake wait. Let me say something. I know there are still feelings between us, and I felt the spark last night just like you did, but I'm not ready to begin anything right now with you or anyone. I am comfortable in my life and my career and I'm not prepared to share that at the moment." Sarah was on a roll. She had practiced this speech earlier in the day on her return trip to the fire scene in case it was needed, and there would be no stopping her until she finished. Except there was a stopping point, and it came with Jake's voice a little louder and more forceful than it was during his greeting.

"Sarah hush! I am not talking about any of that stuff. I need you here at the Life of God Church on South Johnson Street. Are you familiar with the place?"

"Yes I'm familiar. What's going on Jake?" Sarah was taken aback. She was both confused and a little embarrassed at her initial response to his phone call.

"There has been a fire, and Chief Taylor has been taken to the Sheriff's Office for questioning."

"Oh God no! I'm on my way!"

As Sarah pulled into the church parking lot, she saw Jake leaning against one of the fire trucks. When she approached, she could tell that he was distraught. The building was heavily damaged, but the firefighters did a good job of saving what little they could. It was obvious that major renovations would need to take place if it was to be occupied again, but at least the shell was salvageable. Several onlookers had gathered outside the caution tape surrounding the area.

Sarah assumed that a good portion of them were church members who would now be searching for a new place to congregate.

"What the heck happened?" Sarah wanted to be kind and consoling, but the thought of Chief Taylor being held for questioning about a church fire was more than her mind could comprehend at the moment, and she wanted answers.

"Well I am trying to keep an open mind, but it looks bad. Multiple points of origin inside the church with flammable liquid trails coming out the exits, and the entrance door on the side over there has been broken into. It looks like arson although I wouldn't say that to anyone but you without finishing my investigation, but I have to be realistic here. Someone started this thing." Jake seemed both disturbed and agitated while speaking.

"So how does this all relate to Chief Taylor?" Sarah asked with caution since she was afraid of the answer.

"He was here. He was the one that called in the report to 911."

"Well, is that necessarily a bad thing?" Sarah wanted to know.

"There was no reason for him to be here. Late at night, fifteen miles from his house and he just happens upon a fire so soon after losing Cole? That doesn't sound plausible to me at all!"

"Yeah, it does sound pretty bad." Sarah added. "And a church no less. It might be a place to lash out against after what he just went through. Most people tend to question long-held beliefs after such a tragedy, but do you really think the chief capable of something like this?"

"A few days ago I would say there would be no way, but now I'm not sure. I'm not sure about much of anything anymore." Sarah could see the toll this was taking on him. "I had one of the deputies take him to the Sheriff's Office. I will finish up here and go interview him. Would you go with me?"

"Of course." She placed a hand on his shoulder. The spark was still there for her, and she knew it would take every ounce of strength to keep her feelings in check.

"I appreciate that. I have collected most of the evidence and retrieved samples from several spots. I'm sure they will test positive for accelerants. I also have fingerprints. One was taken off of a crowbar lying to the side of the entry door that was busted open. It shouldn't take long to run them through the system and see if we get a hit. Whoever did this didn't seem too worried about concealing the crime."

"It does look that way." Sarah added. "Are you ready to go speak with the chief now?"

"Almost. I need to talk with the guys here first to get their perspective on what happened. They should be finished cleaning everything up by now."

Demon Fire

"Okay, I'm right here with you." Jake had relaxed a little. He knew Sarah was there only professionally, but it was good to have a partner by his side while he navigated through the second investigation in as many nights.

The two walked to an ambulance that had been staging at the scene. A stretcher was outside with a young firefighter sitting down getting his face bandaged.

"What do we have here?" Jake asked as they approached.

"What we have is a dummy that doesn't listen!" Jake turned and saw Fire Captain Sam Nesbit standing off to the side. "Yeah, I told this kid to check his equipment before we went inside. He just decided not to listen. Isn't that true?" He was speaking toward Firefighter Terry Wade as the bandages were being applied.

"Yeah, I guess it was kind of stupid, but no harm done. It's just a flesh wound." The tension in the captain's voice was not present in Terry's. The difference was probably the fact that Captain Nesbit had worked many years with Chief Taylor, and he was on edge because of the events of the last couple of nights. Terry on the other hand was a probationary firefighter with only a few months on the job. His interaction with the chief had consisted of a hiring interview and casual hellos during their rare encounters. He was young and undaunted by the norms and traditions that should be followed, and was merely happy to play in the fire for a while.

Jake saw the big grin on the probie's face and knew the needed information would not come from him so turning to Captain Nesbit Jake began with his go-to question. "Captain can you tell me what happened when you arrived?"

"Yeah, looked like a normal everyday fire on arrival. Smoke and flame was venting out the back side. We made an interior attack, but it was a tough battle once we got inside. It was an unusual fire to say the least. Not sure if I have seen flames dancing around like that before. Every time we would hit the flames in one spot another area would light back up. We were chasing our tails in there. Finally we had to pull out and go defensive. We only had a limited time anyway with that large ceiling span you know."

"What about Chief Taylor?" Jake inquired.

"He was here when we pulled up. He was giving us directions and had already finished the walk-around so we had an idea of the situation. He was a big help, and I'm glad he was with us. The side door over there had been forced open already. Other than that there's not a lot to tell. Just a bit of a strange fire if you ask me."

Jake had a few more questions, but he did not gain much more information. He and Sarah decided to go to the Sheriff's Office hoping the interview with the chief would shed light on what happened and why he was at the church to begin with. As they traveled together in Jake's vehicle, Sarah brought up what was still on both of their minds - what the captain said about the fire.

"A strange fire?" Sarah said.

"Yeah, I picked up on that too. And the flames dancing around? This sounds about as weird as the cabin fire."

"I know. And Captain Nesbit has never been one to exaggerate." Sarah added. "These past two nights have been just too much."

"They have been, and it's not going to get any better having to interview the chief again. I don't want to be overly suspicious, but..." Jake's voice trailed off as Sarah finished the thought for him.

"Do you think he might have been trying to take his anger out on God?"

"That's exactly what I think. I'm trying to go into this with an open mind though, and I need you to help me with that if you could. Especially when we're talking with him. If he had nothing to do with this and I'm too confrontational, then he would never forgive me, and I would never forgive myself."

"I understand. I'll do the best I can, but you might have to look out for me as well because this does not look good for the chief."

Jake diverted to the lab as they entered the Sheriff's Office. There he left the fingerprint samples with the intake officer. After advising what the nature of the investigation entailed and the importance of getting the information to him as soon as possible, Jake and Sarah proceeded to the investigation wing which was one of several sections that made up the interior of the building. Chief Taylor was sitting in a small conference room next to the cubicles the investigators used as their office space. Jake and Sarah entered and sat across from him at the center table.

"Well Jake, you seem to be making a habit of coming to see me. I guess I am getting the VIP treatment by us meeting in here instead of one of the interview rooms." The chief's demeanor stayed calm and collected as he spoke.

"I never liked those little rooms much, anyway. They always seem like they are straight out of a crime show or something." Jake said as the chief began the conversation.

"So I guess you want to know what I was doing out in the middle of the night so far from home watching a church burn."

"That is a question we had on our minds. I assume there is a good reason, but I have to hear it from you." Jake was trying to be as professional as possible, but it was difficult with all the emotions flowing through him. He could

Demon Fire

not believe he was sitting here interviewing his fire chief about an arson fire.

"Well to tell you the truth I don't know what the heck I was doing there. More than that, I don't even know how I got there." Jake had wondered about the transportation too. The firefighters said there were no vehicles in the area when they arrived, and Jake had seen nothing that indicated how the chief got to the church. "All I know is that I woke up in a daze standing in the middle of the sanctuary with smoke all around me."

"You woke up inside the church?" Jake exclaimed. He did not make a habit of interrupting people during an interview, but this statement was unexpected, and he wanted to clarify what he had just heard.

"Yes, that's exactly what I did. I woke up. I know it sounds strange, but I don't know how else to describe it. The last thing I remember was you calling to check on me Jake. You were updating me on how things were going. I was barely paying attention. My mind had been in a fog all day and the headaches I kept having were horrible, but I do remember your call. It was literally the last thing – until I woke up standing in the middle of a fire. It was hot, but the smoke hadn't lowered so I was able to get out with only a slight burn to my hand." They had not noticed the bandaging on his fingertips until the chief pointed it out. "There was an open door to the side, so I made it to safety fairly quickly. I had my phone in my pocket so I called 911 and reported it. The fire spread fast, and I'm sure there was accelerant used. The guys got there and saved some of the structure, though I am sure it will take a long time to repair the building, if that's even possible. I apologize if I'm rambling. It's just that ever since I found myself in the middle of that church I feel like a new man. The fog I was in yesterday has been lifted, and my headaches are gone. I have never felt as strange as I have since the cabin fire. It couldn't have been because of the stress of losing Cole because that pain is still there, but my mind seems free now - somehow."

"I'm glad you are feeling better, and I appreciate you being so candid with us." Jake said.

"Well I want to know what happened tonight, probably more than you do. I don't like the idea of losing hours of my memory so I am willing to help in any way I can. Even if it means finding out that I did something wrong." There was a pause and Jake shifted in his seat. Chief Taylor looked at him then Sarah then down at his hands lying folded on the table. "Do you think I started that fire Jake?"

Jake shifted in his chair again. "I think you might have." The Chief's head dropped a little further. "There was no reason for you to be there. No one else was around. You are distraught over losing Cole. You were in the church at the time of the fire. It just doesn't look good. Now I'm not certain of this. There could be an explanation for everything, but with you not remembering, I will have to fill in the blanks somehow. The door you exited was broken into, and there was a crowbar discarded close by. I pulled fingerprints, and we are running them now. I'm also going to need your phone. I want to retrace your calls and see if I can figure out your transportation to the church."

"Yeah that's not a bad idea." The Chief reached into his pocket and brought out a cell phone which he pushed across the table to Jake.

Jake gazed at the phone and then asked. "Are you sure you want to be this cooperative? I mean I appreciate you being honest with me, and I need to know what went on tonight, but this is pretty serious."

"I know Jake. Look, I lost Cole last night. There is nothing worse this life can throw at me. But that being said - I might have started the fire at that church. If I did, I can't remember it, so it would not have been a conscious decision. You know me, and you know my situation. I trust you to find out what happened and to do the right thing no matter what that might be. The chief's eyes suddenly darted away as he stared at the adjacent wall. He was not trying to hide the fact that something was on his mind, but his interviewers were willing to wait and let him collect his thoughts. Still not looking either one in the eye he asked a question that he already knew the answer to. "You aren't going to let me leave here tonight are you?"

Jake was not prepared for this, but he should have assumed that Chief Taylor knew there was enough probable cause for an arrest.

"No, I'm afraid that you will have to stay at least overnight. I don't doubt the fact that you can't remember anything. I know that traumatic events can play havoc with people's minds, but I can't take the chance of sending you home until everything gets sorted out. If you did black out and start that fire then who's to say that it won't happen again? I would just feel better knowing you were secure tonight at least."

"I understand Jake. I'm a little concerned myself. If it was me, then my mind and body can act without me even realizing. That is a scary thought. I know they'll treat me well here tonight. It's really okay. I can cry myself to sleep here just as well as at home."

Jake and Sarah left the conference room with heavy hearts. The tragedy of the cabin fire was now compounded by the fact that their friend was sitting in jail. Before leaving they stopped back by the lab. The chief's prints were on file because of his public safety job which made it simple to confirm that they were a match to the ones pulled from the crowbar.

"I guess we should have figured that would be the results." Sarah was stating the obvious, but she wanted to break the tension in the car.

"I was still holding out hope, but I guess it's not surprising." Jake stated in agreement. "He was at the scene for no reason, the door was broken into, and now his fingerprints are on a crowbar sitting next to that same door, he just lost his kid and he admits to blacking out. I spoke with the members of the church who were present, and there doesn't seem to be any other suspects. I don't see anything that wouldn't point to the chief?"

"We're on the same page then. First of all he is your main suspect. There is no way around that, and second he does need to be in jail tonight. It breaks my heart especially with Cole's death hanging over him, but if everything happened the way he said then there is nothing that would stop another fire from occurring."

"I feel the same. Thank you so much for being here with me on this. I'm not sure if I could do it alone. Do you want to stop and get something to eat? There are a few diners open this time of night." Jake asked.

Sarah was still cautious about her feelings getting the best of her, and she was ready to put a lid on anything that might send the wrong signals. "No Jake. It's late, and neither one of us has had much sleep. I think I will head home and get some rest."

"Ok. I agree." Jake did not agree. He did not want her to leave, but he felt it best to go along with what she wanted. The two parted ways after arriving back at the church. There were no promises of checking in once home, and a quick goodbye hug was all there was before departure. At the house Jake showered and settled in for what he hoped would be a good rest for the few hours that remained before it would be time to arise and tackle the world again.

Chapter 7
Radiant Heat

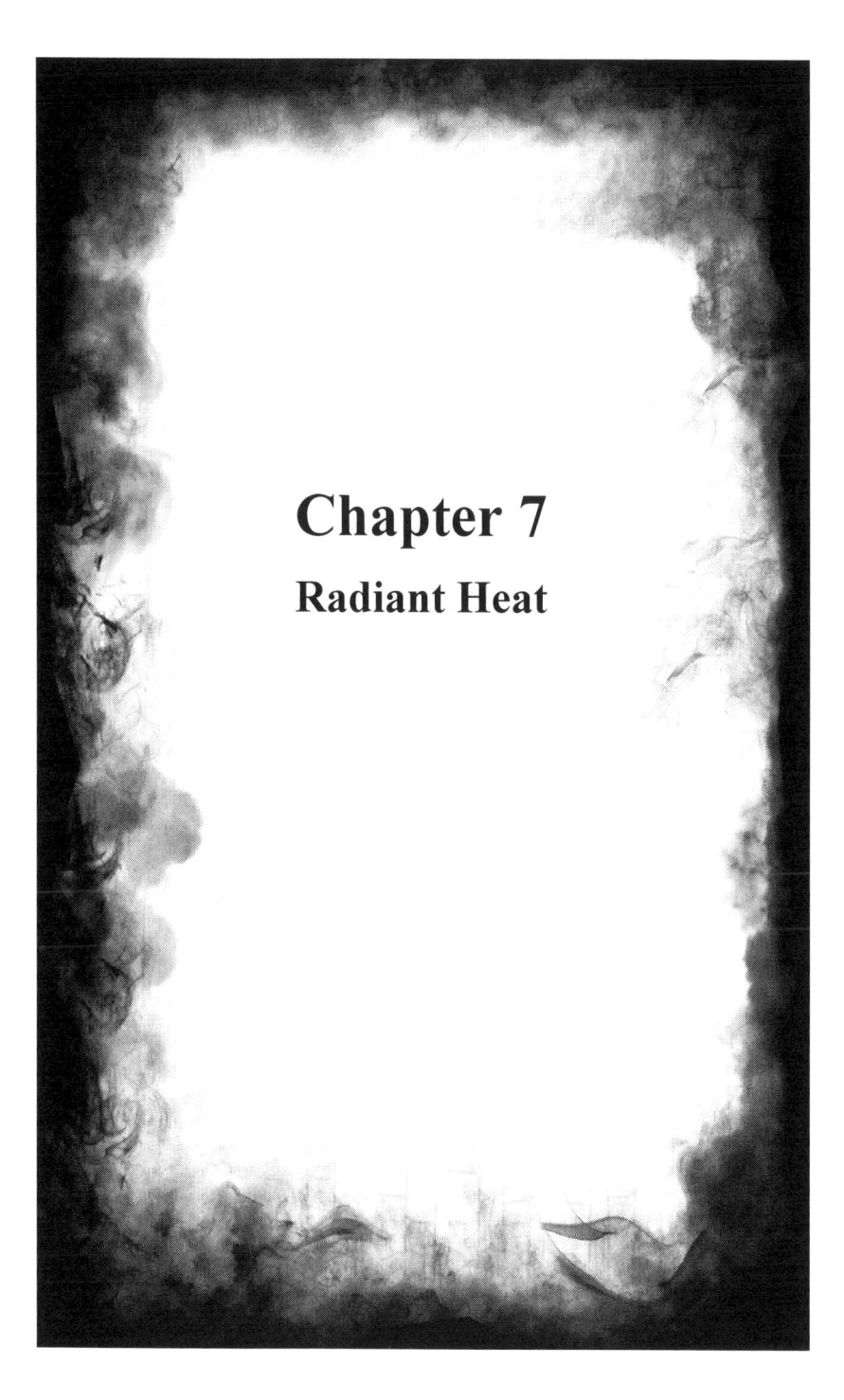

Chris Cumbie

Demon Fire

Sarah spent the remainder of the night at home in restful bliss. The dreams that came were pleasant, and the next morning she actually thought one of them might have been about Jake. She chastised herself for it at first, but then realized that just because she was suppressing feelings did not mean that those feelings were not there subconsciously. The morning was turning out to be normal for her with the daily routine well in effect when her phone rang with a call from dispatch. After the call she took a quick shower, and then hurried out the door. She had been notified of a fire scene on the border of her county and Deer Creek although not much information had been received from the 911 operator other than the address. The fire was extinguished quickly, but there seemed to be a suspicious nature to it so Sarah had been called in. As she pulled onto the scene her heart skipped a beat as she gazed upon the sign outside welcoming visitors to the First Christian Church of Newton. Two church fires in adjacent counties less than twelve hours apart was an unusual occurrence and very suspicious. Her first instinct was that Chief Taylor must be innocent. Someone burned this church, and with him being locked safely away, then another perpetrator must be at fault. The joy was short lived however. She knew the evidence pointed toward the chief setting the earlier fire, and just because another church had burned close by did not change that fact. Sarah decided to put the last couple of days out of her thoughts and not let it cloud her judgment. She had a fire to investigate, and she was determined to go into it with an unbiased opinion. As she approached the structure, however, her mind got thrown for another loop. Sitting on the tailboard of one of the engines was Firefighter Terry Wade.

"Terry! What are you doing here?" Sarah asked. He still had on his fire department station gear, and the bandage from the night before could be seen on his face to go along with a new bandage covering his hand.

"I'm not really sure." Terry stated while shaking his head. "I just kinda woke up here. I know that sounds dumb, but I woke up standing in the lobby. The place was on fire so I got outside to get away from the heat. I have no idea what I am doing here or even how I arrived."

"Well, why don't you tell me what you do know? Is there anything you can remember?" Sarah asked. Her mind was spinning at the familiar sounding description of what Terry was stating.

"Let me see. I got back to the station last night after the fire. I helped clean everything up, took a shower and jumped into the bed for a quick nap before it was time to go home. I had a splitting headache, so I didn't think it would be easy to fall asleep, but I passed out the moment my head hit the pillow. Honestly that is the last thing I remember until I woke up here. It's definitely weird, but at least my headache's gone now."

The innocent grin was still on Terry's face as he spoke. Sarah had no concern for grins or body language though. She focused on the words that were just spoken. The words which copied the ones spoken the night before by Chief Taylor. She was confused. The idea of two churches burning so close together in such a short time period seemed easy for her to chalk up to coincidence, but hearing the two similar stories could not be reasoned away. Sarah's mind raced as she tried to figure out her next move. Being a seasoned investigator meant that she should start with the fire itself, but that was not the path she wanted to take this time. She knew what the fire would tell her. It was an arson and Terry was the one that started it. The firefighters would say the fire and smoke and sounds were strange. They would say something had been different about it, and she didn't care about any of that now. What she needed to find out was why two separate people were blacking out and starting fires. Of course the possibility that Terry and the chief collaborated with each other to start these fires might be an option, but that was not very likely. It was a question that had to be answered though so that would be her first step, and the fire itself would have to wait. The fire crews would tape off the area and hold the scene until she could get back. They would not understand her need to leave, but that was not her concern. Something strange was happening, and she needed to determine what it was as soon as possible.

    A phone call to Jake was necessary. She assumed he would try to rest up that morning, but she was on a mission and he was part of this journey - sleep or no sleep. During the call she filled him in on everything that had happened with her church fire and Firefighter Wade. Jake was shocked, which she expected. His empirical mind would not wrap around her wanting to postpone the investigation of the latest church fire. He assumed there had to be a logical reason behind everything and that the answers would be found in the fire. Sarah disagreed, and since this fire belonged to her, she would do things her way. Jake had been around Sarah long enough to know that once she had decided on something like this, there was no use arguing so he decided to follow her lead.

    She wanted to take their suspects to meet Justin Maxwell at the Elkins City Police Department. Justin had a reputation as the best polygraph examiner in the area. He began his career as a military intelligence officer, and after retirement brought his interrogation skills to civilian law enforcement. Detective Maxwell was well respected in his field, and once he had a subject hooked to his machine, the truth would always reveal itself. He would even test his fellow officers with no one ever coming close to beating him or his machine.

The trip to Elkins would take approximately twenty minutes from Sarah's location and about thirty for Jake. They decided to travel separately and have Chief Taylor and Firefighter Wade meet them at Detective Maxwell's office with transportation provided by deputies from the respective jurisdictions. The tests would be voluntary since neither one could be compelled to take part. Chief Taylor agreed to the test right away. He did not hide his excitement about the prospect of finding answers to the blacked out time in-between his house and the fire scene, and the thought of getting away from his cell was pleasing. The time spent locked up and alone was worse than he thought it would be since the only thing he could do was sit and think. And the only thing he could think about was Cole. Firefighter Wade had a few questions when approached with the suggestion of a polygraph test, but he did not oppose since Sarah thought it was a good idea.

Sarah arrived first and was waiting as Jake entered Detective Maxwell's office ignoring customary pleasantries. "What the heck is going on Sarah?" His animosity was obvious, but both Sarah and the detective knew it was not directed toward them. They considered the pressure Jake found himself under having to investigate the death of Cole and then arrest the very man who had hired him and who had suffered such a tragic loss. "Another church fire and another fire department member saying they blacked out? There is no way we are going to make any sense of this!" Jake stood in the threshold of the office doorway, and as he finished speaking, his gaze shifted from Sarah to the detective.

"Hi Jake, it's good to see you although I wish it were under better circumstances." Detective Maxwell said. His eyes did not wander away from Jake's while speaking. Jake took control of his emotions and realized how unprofessional it must look to storm into the detective's office like that.

"Hey Justin, sorry about that. It's been brutal the past couple of days. I appreciate you fitting us in."

"That's not a problem. I realize the stress you are dealing with, and I am glad to help. Maybe Libby will have some answers for you." Libby was the detective's pet name for his lie detector. Everyone thought it strange to humanize a piece of equipment, but considering the amount of time the man and machine spent together over the years no one ever questioned it. "Tell me what exactly you two are hoping to get out of the questioning?" Each investigation whether it is an arson, homicide or simple burglary has its own set of parameters for questions. The obvious queries, such as whether or not a subject had committed the crime, were normally broached as well as any which might give credence to a possible alibi. The questions Jake and Sarah had agreed upon, after some discussion, revolved around the time before the two fires and the supposed blacked-out areas of their memories. Since the two church fire investigations were so similar they decided to keep the questions the same for both the chief and Firefighter Wade, neither of which would know the other was being interviewed.

Chief Taylor arrived first and met the trio in the interview area. The chauffer was a young deputy who, to the relief of Jake and Sarah, had not used handcuffs during transport. This was a professional courtesy that had been afforded to the chief by the sheriff due to his standing in the community, and it was appreciated by all involved. Detective Maxwell led Chief Taylor into a separate area to proceed with the test after everyone completed their hellos. The chief seemed in good spirits, which comforted both Jake and Sarah who stayed behind in the office to wait. Once they were alone, Sarah moved her chair slightly closer to Jake.

"How are you holding up?" The answer was obvious since Jake looked like he had been put through the ringer.

"I'm doing okay. It just seems like this roller coaster ride we are on will not slow down. Every time I think we are at a stopping point something else crazy happens. I am not used to all of this chaos. I like things by the book and in order, especially with the fires I investigate. Even the most complex fires we work have a simple beginning and a definite end. There is always a progression of the facts that might not be easy to find at first, but they always end up presenting themselves. I am just tired of these unanswered questions. That and the fact we are so emotionally involved in this case. It's just wearing on me, and I know it's difficult for you as well." Jake reached his hand over and patted Sarah on the knee. It was an innocent gesture, but it impressed Sarah that someone could go through so much pain and still care about her wellbeing.

"I'm confused like you are. The same thoughts running through your head are running through mine. I feel confident we are about to get answers from this test though so that is at least something positive to look forward to."

"I agree. I'm hoping that some clarity will come from the questions. I just wish we could sit in on it." Jake said.

"You know the detective has his own way of doing things. He said he wanted to be alone with both the chief and Terry and that he didn't want to fill us in until they both had been questioned. It sucks to just sit out here, but he is the best at what he does. We have to go with his instinct on this one. We can always listen to the recordings after the fact."

The two stayed in the office during the chief's questioning and reminisced about old times. It was nice that both were able to take their minds off of the situation for a while. In fact they were both laughing and cutting up with each other when Detective Maxwell arrived.

"We are finished." The detective said.

"How did he do?" Sarah asked.

"Well, *they* did fine. I have finished up with the chief and Firefighter Wade."

"Really? We have been in here that long?" Asked Jake.

"Yep. I ended with the chief about the time that Terry arrived. I sent one out the back as I brought the other through the side, and I am done with both."

"Wow, I guess we lost track of time." Sarah said.

"That's not necessarily a bad thing. You two have been under an incredible amount of strain the past couple of days. It's nice that you could have a moment of levity. Maybe even work on rekindling feelings if possible. I always thought you two would make a good couple. Too bad it didn't work out." Detective Maxwell had a look on his face like someone that knows something others do not. The words and smile were noticed by both Jake and Sarah. The detective had a way of reading people. It was what he had been trained to do, and he had perfected the skill during his professional career. The two looked at each other a little embarrassed, Sarah more so than Jake since she had been determined to keep her feelings in check. Now her emotions were so obviously visible that they were noticed by others. The awkward moment passed and Jake spoke.

"So detective, I assume you have answers for us."

"I do." The detective said. "First, I would like to know what you two think about this whole situation. I mean you have the most tragic of fire deaths. You have the fire chief, who we all care for and respect. You have a starry eyed firefighter, and you have fires breaking out all over the place. So what does your gut tell you?"

Sarah began to speak then stopped herself suddenly and looked at Jake. She felt that he had more at stake in this so she would defer to him, but he was not having any of that. This would be a joint effort.

"Go ahead Sarah." Jake said. "This is our investigation not just mine."

"Okay, well detective, we laid out the facts of the case to you before. I believe Jake and I are on the same page with our thinking which contains more confusion than confidence. Nothing about any of these fires has been normal. The way the fires were described by the on scene firefighters, the way they began, spread and acted. The way the chief and Terry recounted how each found themselves at the churches. Someone must not be telling the truth about something. The world of fire just doesn't work this way."

"I understand your frustration." The detective had moved to his desk and leaned back in his oversized leather chair. The chair was believed by his colleagues to be too big for its surroundings, but he didn't care. It was comfortable, and Detective Maxwell had never been one to care much about what other people thought. "First of all I know very little about fire investigations. You two are the experts so I am going to take your word that these fires were out of the ordinary. I can tell you definitively about the two suspects in the case though. There was no deception from either one."

Both Jake and Sarah were surprised by this statement. They didn't have much of an idea about what was behind the fires and the relation of the chief and Terry to them, but a blanket assertion from the detective about their truthfulness was not what they would have predicted.

"They were both telling the truth?" Jake could not hide the confusion in his voice. "How is that possible? They have the same story about two different church fires, and both talked about blacking out. That's crazy."

"Crazy, unexplainable, outlandish. Yes, you could say it is a bit out of the ordinary to have this kind of scenario, but believe me when I tell you. They are both telling the truth. There was not a shred of deceit in anything they said. The blackout spells, the waking up at the fire scene, the headaches beforehand and feeling great afterwards, it's all true. Neither one of them had any false readings during the tests, and even without the machine I have no doubt that they were being anything other than honest."

"But how is that possible?" Sarah had leaned forward in her chair.

"That is a question that the two of you must answer. I have given you all the facts as I know them. I will give you a piece of advice though if you might indulge me." The statement trailed off in anticipation of a response.

"Please." Sarah began. "Anything you could do to help would be appreciated. I'm not sure that either one of us knows where to go from here." She looked at Jake who had a despondent look on his face.

"Well, you know a little about my history. My intelligence career with the military took me all over the world, and I had the opportunity to see and experience things that most people would never dream of. Most of the work I did was not extraordinary, but now and then a case would come along that seemed to defy the logical way things are supposed to work. It was never anything obvious, but maybe an unexplained way a person died or a group of people finding themselves in a less than conventional situation. My mind was focused to look for out of the ordinary situations and believe me, I found them. The job you have done over the years is commendable, but it has been confined to a localized area. The world out there is a strange place, and I have found that it doesn't always follow the rules." There was a pause in the conversation as Detective Maxwell's gaze lifted slightly to the ceiling and his mind seemed to wander as he was reminiscing.

"So what does this all mean to us?" Jake asked.

"I'm not sure what it means to you Jake, but my advice is to take a break from logic for a while. Start thinking outside the box on this one. Possibly way outside. Do not limit yourselves to the normal processes you would follow or the same avenues you would normally travel. Open your minds to new possibilities and really look at what is out there. I have done this on multiple occasions during my lifetime when the answer to a question was not readily available, and more times than not I have been led in the right direction by doing so."

Jake and Sarah sat quietly for several seconds after the detective finished. Finally Sarah spoke as she rose from her seat with Jake following suit.

"Thanks for your help detective. I appreciate your advice although I'm not sure what to do with it at the moment."

"Well you don't have to know what to do. Sometimes it is better that you don't, but while I am giving out free advice - there is great energy between the two of you. I'm not only talking about the working relationship. There is a chemistry there that one doesn't have to be a trained investigator to see."

The two looked at each other. Jake had a feeling of justification that his feelings were not in vain, and Sarah with a sense of dread that her determination might be waning. They both thanked the detective for his help and departed.

"So what do you think?" Jake asked once they arrived back to the parking lot.

"I don't know. I hoped that we would leave here with answers and instead we are leaving with more questions. I guess I need to go back to my church fire. Maybe digging through debris will ground me a little, get me back to reality."

"That sounds like a good idea. Do you need me to help you?" Jake asked.

"No, I will be fine. I think some solitude will do me good. If I had it my way, I would head to the old Kaleton Hill Trail for a mind clearing run."

"I got ya. I'm going home myself. I should clear my brain and find a way to refocus. Do you mind calling later tonight with an update on what you find at the church?"

"Sure Jake. I will call you. Take care of yourself. Hopefully we'll come up with a path forward somehow."

Chapter 8
The Fire Within

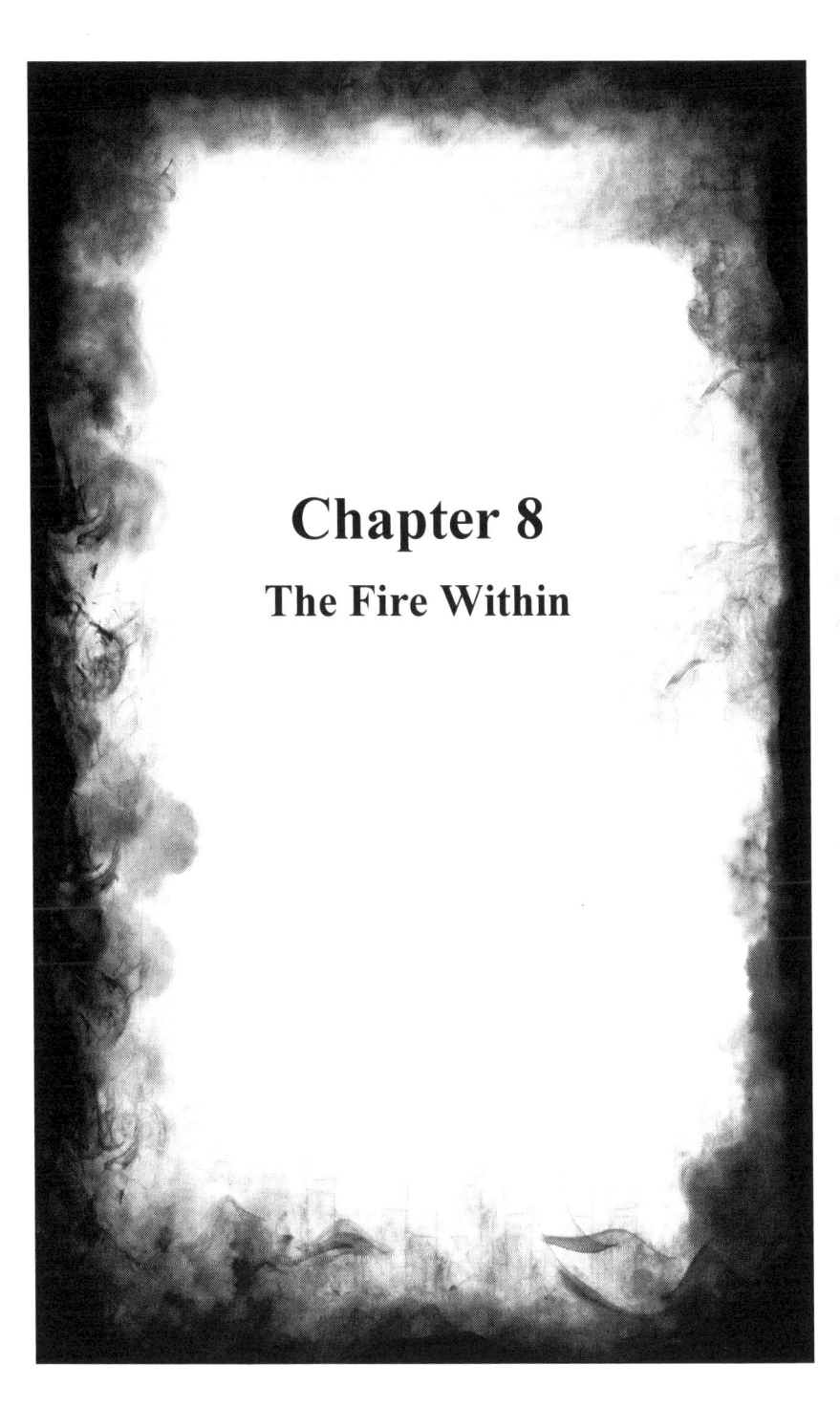

Chris Cumbie

Demon Fire

David had been in charge on and off for the past several hours, and the familiarity with his surroundings and how his host body would react to certain stimuli grew by the minute. He had been in full control during times of unconsciousness, but now he had the ability to command aspects of life while his host was conscious as well. Memories were checked when needed, such as when a visitor had arrived that morning to check on the welfare of his host. David recognized the individual as one of the visitors at the hospital although he was too busy trying to take in all of the new experiences at the time to remember who he was. The visit gave little concern, but a potential obstacle presented itself as the memory showed a glimpse of who this new person was. The visitor's job responsibilities included investigating intentionally set fires and arresting the guilty party. A person such as this could hamper his efforts, so during the brief exchange between the two a mental note was made of the person's facial features and mannerisms. David would make it a priority to remember this individual since an incarcerated host would be a distinct disadvantage and must not be allowed.

As the day grew longer, and the afternoon arrived, a test of David's abilities began. Chief Taylor had remained in a state of languor, so it was easy for David to take over whenever he chose. He came to the front of the mind and took the view of his host's eyes. The appendages moved freely with only a thought, although it took a moment to become oriented. First the arms lifted up and down, and the feet moved side to side. Then the focus shifted to the walk. The walk would be one of the more important parts of the equation since well focused steps would help keep attention from coming his way. A person's gait is a distinguishing factor, and an awkward one would be as noticeable as a change in voice.

As David figured, the host contained a plethora of information on what must be done to succeed at his plan. The first task, however, was to become presentable. The clothes had to be changed, and the occupied body needed to be cleaned. Filth would be an unwanted attribute, especially for a man as well known as his unwitting partner. David led his shared body to the bedroom where the surroundings were much more comfortable than the flattened bedrolls he had been accustomed to in the former life. A change of clothes was set on the bed for later use including a pair of slacks and a button-up shirt from the closet, as well as socks and underwear from the dresser. Shoes were found in a corner, and as David used his host's eyes to scan over the items of clothing, he determined that the chosen garments matched the proper style and weather for his outing. Next on the agenda would be the shower.

The equipment providing water from the outside source was unfamiliar but not difficult to operate. Once the apparatus was deciphered, the water against his borrowed skin became an interesting sensation, and the droplets of liquid raining down on his new body from the shower head were quite pleasurable. The warmth ran through his entire nervous system and the feeling after so many years of nothingness was so good that David temporarily forgot the purpose of this procedure. Over time, as the water began to cool, he reached for the soap and quickly lathered up the body. New sensations arrived with the hands running over exposed skin, but focus had been regained, and he finished the task without pause.

Dressed in the pre-selected clothes, David made his way to the phone. The device was not familiar to him although plenty of direction lived in the host's mind to figure out the inner-workings. The instrument had a section designated for data retrieval so a search was initiated, but the first several keywords did not produce the desired results. After a more thorough scouring of the memory the number to Gerald's Taxi Service and Auto Repair Shop was found and dialed. The amazing technology of this new world he occupied was not lost on David. The information access, the communication abilities as well as the electricity that lit up the night were all strange and exciting aspects of life that would have been nice to indulge in. For a brief moment, a sense of longing for a time when the mind and soul were not corrupt crept into his consciousness. This notion had to be subdued, however. Taking time to explore and enjoy all of the new experiences would interfere and be a detriment to the plan so the thought was ignored as he settled in to wait for the arrival of transportation.

While waiting for the conveyance, a determination was made to provide sustenance to the host. There had been no nourishment since the night of Cole's death, and a fear became prevalent that weakness could overtake him at any moment. A quick trip to the kitchen provided a quantity of food that he had never imagined in the previous time period. Bread, fruit and meats along with vegetables and other various foods that were not recognizable filled the cabinets. David could have spent hours tasting all the new delicacies. The flavors cascading across his host's tongue were experienced vividly by the passenger. It would have been easy to indulge, but he would not allow himself the pleasure.

Instead he ate the minimum amount to sustain through the night. A surge of energy arrived after the brief meal and David's excitement grew at the prospect of his plan unfolding after all the years of waiting. The details of the plan were sparse, but the framework of what needed to be accomplished had always been present. Now that the time for action had come, a sense of urgency arose.

After several minutes of waiting passed, David noticed that he had been pacing back and forth through the house. It seemed to him like patience would be an attribute of plenty, but the anticipation and anxiousness was almost more than he could bear. There was no more planning and no more studying of memories to keep him occupied. The time to enact his plan was now, but the waiting was an annoyance. Just as the mind started to lose what grip it had on sanity, however, a strange noise came from outside the house.

The taxicab sat at the curb with the driver honking the horn impatiently. A sense of relief wafted over David as he grabbed the host's wallet, which hopefully contained the proper amount of currency needed for the ride, and then headed outside. The night air was crisp but felt good to the skin. Many of the sensations that might have brought discomfort at another time were tolerated now because of the focus of attention on the grander purpose and the need to feel anything after going so long without.

As David approached, the driver, who was mistakenly assumed to be Gerald, spoke.

"Hey buddy. Hop on in and let's figure out where we're headin."

The dialect was thick with a local accent that had not been heard before, but David understood the words so he entered through the back door as the memories had suggested.

"I would like to go to the Life of God Church on South Johnson Street." David said.

The driver, who according to the identification hanging from the front air vent was named Cory not Gerald, had a look of confusion on his face. It could be assumed that a normal confused demeanor followed this particular individual, but David knew there had been something wrong with his statement. The words were correct, but the tone and delivery lacked clarity with everything spoken too slow and pronounced with too much effort. The practice of mind control and muscle manipulation provided an acceptable appearance, but the art of speaking had not been practiced. David realized that he had not uttered a single word since the fateful day when the nothingness began. A shiver traveled through his host's body as the memories of that time flooded back.

"Hey man. Are you drunk or something? I don't care if you are, but I like to know who I'm gonna be riding around with."

Cory's statement brought reality back to the forefront, and David collected himself and tried to focus. The words that came still sounded off, but they were at least understandable.

"No. I'm sick." It was a simple assertion, but one that appeased the driver.

"Okay man. No problem. Just don't sneeze on me or anything. Life of God Church it is."

The drive was short and uneventful, but as the vehicle pulled into the parking lot, the driver began a series of concerning questions.

"It looks like we are the only ones here fella. Are you supposed to be meeting someone or something?" David was unprepared for an interrogation, and he had no good answer. "I mean, I don't mind dropping you off or anything. It's just that you don't look like no preacher, and it doesn't look like they are having services tonight. I'm not trying to get in your business, but I don't want no police comin' around asking me questions about some guy I dropped off."

Of course David knew the situation must have looked suspicious, and there was no way of coming up with a good lie. Even if he had an excuse to give the man, the difficulty in speaking would make it impossible to convince him that the falsehood was true. His energy sank as he realized the plan was about to be shattered before it began. His mind retreated and dove straight into the memories to find an answer as fast as possible. A long pause in answering the driver's question would be a catastrophe. A decision would be made soon whether to turn around and take his passenger back to the house or even to the police station for questioning. Luckily, however, a memory produced a way out. His host had dealt with these kinds of issues before while interacting with certain less than desirable members of the community who he would come across while carrying out his official duties. Using this information now might be the only way to salvage the night and maybe the entire operation.

"Tip!" David almost yelled the word as he reached for the wallet in his pants pocket.

"Darn right tip." The driver offered back. "And I'm talkin' about a good one too!"

A handful of cash appeared through the small opening in the car partition. David had no clue how much he handed over, but the wide eyes on the receiving end indicated it was more than enough.

"Well buddy. You don't know how to talk, and I'm pretty sure you are up to no good, but you do know how to give a fine tip. Best of luck to ya."

David exited the vehicle and watched as the taxicab faded from view. The church was dimly lit, but enough light was available to operate. The memories had suggested a shed behind the main building would offer the needed tools for the job. As David approached, he could tell that the entrance was locked with some kind of exterior latching device. The clasp looked formidable, and if a sturdy door and frame had been attached, it might have caused an issue, but the shed was old and in disrepair. A strong kick made an adequate opening, and the decision not to bring his own equipment was vindicated.

The inside was not spacious, but someone had taken the time to organize the surroundings with shelving and storage bins which made the most of almost every square inch of room. In the center sat a lawnmower used for the church grounds. Tools were found near the exterior door and lawn equipment had been neatly placed along the walls. The host's knowledge was put to use, and a can of flammable liquid was the first item chosen. Plenty of gas cans lay about, but luckily for David the church had purchased a portable generator that was fed by a container of diesel fuel. Gas would work well to help start and spread a fire, but the volatility of the product would pose a danger to the host. Although there was no sense of care for the occupied vessel, he needed the host and it must be kept from harm. Next a stack of newspapers sitting beside a grill was noticed with a lighter lying on top. David assumed that a fire starter would be found in the church since there had been a memory of candles being present, but finding one here would save him from having to search once inside.

All the items were gathered and taken to the side door of the church. This door was more substantial so David made one last trip to the shed and returned with a crowbar. Little traffic had been seen passing on the road, and there were no houses close by. The pastor's residence was not on the property so a need for quiet did not present itself as the chosen tool slammed in between the door and frame. A large crack ran a foot in each direction out from where the crowbar landed. The second hit broke half of the frame off and the door popped open. A burglar alarm was not present so nothing but silence met his entry. The door opened into the sanctuary, and David paused as he entered. Emotion bubbled up at the site of his surroundings. The place of worship had once been a welcoming place, but now after all the years in solitude the only emotion that remained was hate.

The newspapers were taken to various parts of the room and crumpled up as kindling. A plentiful supply of burnable materials surrounded the area, and the addition of diesel fuel would work nicely for what was in store. Once everything was in place, David placed a hand inside the front pocket of his pants and pulled out the lighter. Kneeling down at a spot at the far side of the room, he flicked his thumb across the flint wheel which made a spark that quickly extinguished. A puzzled look crossed the face of his host as the memory was checked for instructions. After a brief moment the wheel spun once again as the push button was held and the flame lifted.

The eyes fixated on the dancing light as the device fed the flame with a hiss of combustible fuel. A sense of longing arose deep inside, and the temptation to reach out and touch the heat grew strong. Riding the waves of fire in the cabin had been exhilarating, but as he daydreamed, a sudden feeling of dread and fear overtook him. As much as he wanted to dance in the fire before him, the flame was small and its continued life was contingent on his finger holding down a simple button. It was obvious that once the soul transferred, the thumb would release and there was no way to tell what would happen next. David was not interested in finding out so he lowered the lighter to its intended destination. He then lit each area and took a step back to admire his work.

The heat and smoke increased as the flames grew, and as more areas burned so did the satisfaction and the urge to dance crept into his mind once more. This time the thought did not fade like before. The flames were too magnificent to ignore. Just a taste of the freedom of movement, the flow back and forth through the heat was more temptation than he could take.

David moved his borrowed body closer, not thinking of the fact that the heat might become an issue for the host. David was not prepared to back away though, so against the previous better judgment he moved his hand forward. The entire mind focused on this movement, and it was ready to jump at the first chance it had. That moment came as the fingertips brushed softly against the tip of a protruding flame, and before the nervous system instinctively pulled back, David was flowing through a dimension of fire. Joy flowed as the flames danced up the walls and down again.

The rolling movements were recalled from when he had escaped the nothingness. This time was different though. The obliteration of the church and what it meant to David had been magnified by the fact that he was able to promulgate that destruction himself. He was not only traveling through the fire, but he actively controlled it as well. Each charred piece of material was consumed through his direct intervention and this knowledge brought a great amount of pleasure. So much so that time and location were forgotten along with the plan and purpose for being there in the first place. The only thoughts were of the heat and destruction. He was unaware of the passing minutes during this delirium, but at one point he heard a familiar sound beyond the crackling and popping noises of the fire. He tried to remember where he had heard the commotion before. It was not a noise from his past so it must have been a recent recollection. Then he remembered crossing paths with the sound during the first night of freedom. It had originated from fire apparatus arriving at the cabin, and with that realization came the understanding of what the noise meant. People were coming to extinguish the fire.

As this fact occurred to him another issue arose. The host was gone. David searched every inch of the area. Each flame passing around corners looking in between the pews, but nothing was found. Too much time had been spent frolicking with no attention given to the whereabouts or wellbeing of the one who brought him. He must have regained consciousness, realized the danger and escaped.

A mistake such as this was unfathomable. There was no way this could have occurred, but it had. Somehow it had. The pain and misery were irrepressible. The thought that his plan had been foiled so soon after it began was overpowering, and the fury manifested itself as the flames shot through the roof flying off in every direction.

The madness lasted several minutes when suddenly the fire pushed back from the front of the building. Unaware of what was happening David focused on that point of the church as he sent a rush of heat towards the receding flames. For a moment the heat overtook the area, but soon steam could be seen rising in the background. Another wall of fire was sent from a flanking position but that too had little effect. The rage was taking over. Not only was David stuck in the flames with no foreseeable way out, but his power over those same flames seemed to be diminishing, and he was not sure why or how to proceed. All hope drained as the mist rose around him. Then to his amazement, two figures emerged behind the smoke. The couple was dressed in strange garments, but to David they were beautiful creatures because of the optimism they provided. Although the outfits were unusual, the time spent inside of his previous host, and the fact that their presence coincided with the extinguishment of the fire made for an easy determination as to what their purpose was. It was also clear that another opportunity had revealed itself. Two possible host vessels had entered his domain.

The firefighters had brought a pressurized water delivery system that stunted the growth of the flames though it was not a concern now because the expansion of the fire was secondary at this point. All of David's focus turned toward obtaining another host, and all his energy let loose on the two interlopers. The water device flowed while fighting back the onslaught of flames but the heat found weak spots in the liquid as the flames licked at the arms and legs of the firefighters, but a transfer did not occur. Somehow the exterior shell blocked his advances. Undeterred David searched for holes in the armor. There had to be an entryway that could be exploited, and after several seconds he found it. The individual on the working end of the hose seemed well protected. His boots, pants and coat were all in place. The gloves had been pulled tight, and the helmet secured snuggly. A mask of some sort covered the face, and it looked to be intact and protecting properly.

There was one area, however, that looked promising. Around the neck just below the ears appeared to be a thin fabric covering. David concentrated on this point, and as he did so a sliver of skin exposed itself. The patch was a semicircle at the jaw where the mask and the fabric joined. A great opportunity had been presented and it would not be wasted as all efforts were refocused.

"Ow. Dang it!" The words were muffled but discernible.

"Are you okay Wade?"

"Yeah, I'm good Cap. The fire just bit me a little."

"Well suck it up kid. Keep pushing forward. The flames are receding. I think we about have this thing whipped."

Captain Nesbit and Firefighter Wade were partnered on Engine 12 along with Engineer Davis who manned the pump. The captain was normally assigned to a ladder truck at a different station, but he had picked up an extra shift for one of the lieutenants. He was now glad he did. Church fires were always a danger since the large span of the ceiling can easily give way under the heat. A collapse with firefighters inside would be catastrophic so having an experienced person backing up a newbie like Firefighter Wade was helpful.

The fire was in fact dissipating, but staying on the interior of the structure was no longer an option. The Captain's internal clock had gone off, and he knew the fire had burned too long for a crew to stay inside. Firefighter Wade being the new kid full of spunk but little experience didn't want to leave, but he reluctantly followed the orders to pull out. An exterior attack was mounted at that point and as time went by different crews swapped out, and when things slowed down and salvage and overhaul operations reached completion, the Captain found Firefighter Wade being tended to by the standby ambulance team.

"Let me see where it got you." His voice conveyed a tone of both concern and displeasure. He took a cursory glance earlier, as they had come out of the fire the first time, and had determined that the damage was minimal, but he wanted to get a closer look now that the scene had calmed down a bit.

Firefighter Wade turned his head and tilted up at the captain's flashlight. A red streak appeared under the light. It was approximately a quarter inch wide and two inches long.

"Well it's not going to kill you, but it might leave a bit of a scar." The Captain said.

"There's nothing wrong with that." Terry surmised. "My face was too pretty, anyway. A little battle scar to roughen the edges won't hurt none." The Captain tried to hide the grin, but it was to no avail. Everyone laughed at the young firefighter. They all figured him to be a know-it-all kid, but most had been the same way at the beginning of their careers, and at least he had some wit about him.

"Just get that thing bandaged up, and the next time I tell you to check your equipment before you go in I mean check it. The fire will always find a weakness, and if you don't have the hood and mask pulled tight, you are asking for trouble. Now hurry up. It looks like Jake is here. He will want to talk to us."

As the engine pulled into the station Terry was complaining about a headache which was not unusual after a fire. Firefighting can take a lot out of a person. Lugging around sixty pounds of gear and equipment while crawling through an oven wears on a person's body. This pain seemed worse than normal, however, so after the hoses and tools had been cleaned and the truck restocked he went straight to the shower and then the bunk room. One of the aspects of station life that the new firefighter had not gotten used to was the sleeping arrangements. The fire station he was assigned to housed one engine and one heavy rescue which placed six guys piled up in the same bedroom. Between everyone going to bed at different times, the various calls during the night and the inevitable snoring it was not an easy adjustment.

Tonight was not a normal one though. Terry crawled into his bunk and passed out the moment his head hit the pillow.

The next morning the entire shift was tired from the night before, with most of the crew sleeping until they heard the day shift enter the station. Captain Nesbit had been up at his usual early time and was in the office passing on information to the oncoming lieutenant. Terry was up and moving without too much trouble although more than once he was asked if he was doing okay. He must have looked as rough as he felt, but a quick nod and thumbs up was enough to keep anyone from delving further.

Terry did not have much information to pass along to the next shift because of his position. The Captain handled the station handoff, and the Engineer would manage the truck so as soon as the top of the hour struck Terry was in his car driving through the parking lot. Some of the others meandered to their vehicles as the on-coming crew pulled the fire vehicles out for truck check, but no one seemed to notice when he turned right out of the station instead of left toward his apartment.

He drove five miles down the road struggling to keep the vehicle between the lines and turned left onto a side street that was rarely used by the public. Another thousand feet and then left into the Deer Creek Fire Department Training Complex. The car pulled up to the gate with a jerk as the brakes were depressed harder than necessary. Once he figured out how to put the car in park, Terry got out and unlocked the gate with the key he swiped back at the station. Driving into the complex he saw the needed item underneath a canopy next to the main burn building which was comprised of four interconnected metal shipping containers. Wooden pallets were stacked at the end of one container ready to burn during the training exercises. To ignite the wood, a large propane torch was used, and this is what was needed at the moment. Once the item was loaded into the trunk, he took off again this time heading north in the direction of Johnson County.

David felt confident in his growing abilities to command the new host. The taxi ride he took the night before almost turned disastrous when the driver became suspicious, but now that he was learning the nuances of muscle control, the transportation issue had solved itself. He had kept the learned memories of his previous host during the transfer, which was advantageous since he still had directions to his next target in mind. One issue bothered him however. During the night he had come across the same investigator from the first fire. This person, who everyone called Jake, was progressing in his search for the arsonist and had seemed to key in on David's previous host as a suspect. David's transfers into his hosts had been haphazard at best and foolish at worst. No thought had been put into choosing the first two victims, but he was determined to correct this with the next.

As Firefighter Wade's vehicle pulled into the town of Newton, David was using his host to practice speech patterns by talking to himself. The times he had spoken out loud had been scrutinized, and the last thing he wanted in the future was to bring undue attention his way. The church was in the southern corner of the town square, and since it was still early, and the population consisted predominately of commuters, few people were around. However, keeping a low profile was not of great concern this time, since he would not use the occupied vessel again. He parked next to the church building in the parking lot of a dry cleaning establishment that had yet to open for the day. The binoculars in his hands had more than likely been noted on the fire engine's checklist as missing that morning. Engineer Davis would be questioned about them the next shift, but that would not be a worry for today.

David sat watching for several minutes. A calm attitude was present, and he was actually enjoying himself. The past few days had been a whirlwind of activity, new experiences and awareness, but now he was more confident in his abilities and familiar with the systems of his various hosts' bodies. This confidence gave him a sense of focus and determination that his plan would come to fruition, and he would be able to bring pain to the embodiment of his own suffering. As he watched, his eyes concentrated not on the church itself, but on the attached parsonage. The sun hung high enough in the sky that the area could be seen, but light from the inside of the residence would be the key so the binoculars continued to scan. Suddenly off to the right David saw movement. The inside still was not illuminated, but the blinds of a side room had been opened, and there was Pastor Stephens looking out on the morning. David's heart sank as he gazed upon the pastor and memories began flowing back from the time before the nothingness. He was quick to steady his nerves, however, and quickly regained focus. The pastor wore a robe, which meant that he would not set foot into the actual church until breakfast and possibly a shower. This pastor was a big part of the plan of the day, but the timing had to be precise.

As the man retreated from the window David sprung his host into action. The trunk was opened in an instant as he spun to the back of the car and lifted out the torch. A portable propane tank was attached which weighed about twenty pounds when full, which this one was. The entire contraption with hose and nozzle was awkward to carry, and would have been noticeable to any passerby paying attention. Most people in this new world David found himself in were far from observant though, so he meandered along unbeknownst to anyone. Although there was no crowbar or any other tool readily available, entry into the building did not call for such equipment. The double front doors were constructed of sturdy old wood latched together with wide bands of metal. Going through this entrance would not be the best route since even the most unobservant town member would notice someone breaking down the entrance to a place of worship.

There was, however, a long ramp along the side of the church that led to a separate entranceway. The door at the top of the incline looked substantial. It was oversized, supposedly to help the disabled parishioners enter the building, and although the door would hold up well to a forced entry attempt, there were windows which had been placed on either side that shattered easily as the thrown rock slammed against the glass. A quick flick of the latch on the oversized door and David found himself inside.

The ornate architectural details of this church were impressive. A dozen stained glass windows reached from the floor to the ceiling on each side of the seating area. The rising sun glistened through the separate colored panes making the artwork within gleam with brilliance. David stood in awe of his surroundings. Great brass pipes rose from behind the altar, and although he was unfamiliar with their use, David was still amazed at the craftsmanship that went into them. For a moment he forgot the purpose of being in this place. He harkened back to a simpler time when he found joy in going to church and congregating with others. In his wildest dreams he would have never imagined a place like this. Looking down at the destructive device in his hands broke his daze and made him realize that the joy that once enveloped his life had been veiled with layers of pain and distrust. It was a nice respite to glimpse the love and caring he once enjoyed, but it was a fleeting emotion easily crushed by what the building represented to him now.

As he regained his sense of purpose, a whoosh of gas mixing with the flame exited the nozzle of his torch. Moving quickly, several areas throughout the main part of the church were set ablaze. The propane worked well as the flames ignited each exposed item. They moved with a vengeance up and out over the open spaces easily reaching the ceiling. As the flames increased so did the smoke which was expected and desired. Through his two fire department hosts David had learned of detection instruments located in large occupancies such as this. These devices would be necessary to alert the occupant, and as he moved away to admire his work the smoke alarms began to sound on cue. The ear piercing noise reverberated around the room, and soon his next host would be making an appearance. All his attention focused on the door to the far side of the room where the parsonage entrance was located. Several seconds went by as a sudden fear had him thinking that his calculations on human nature might be off. His next host might not come through the door. He might do any number of unanticipated things that included running away from the fire instead of investigating the noise of the detection devices.

When the doorknob began to turn, however, David's fear subdued, and the journey began. Terry's hand was quickly moved into the flames which then raced across the ceiling and down the opening of the door before him. Exposed fingers curling in around the edge were in perfect position, and as the pastor's hand jerked back, David saw the door slam back against the heat and fire from the other side. He was a passenger once more as he ran from the church with nothing but a robe covering his new body.

Chapter 9
Kindling

Chris Cumbie

Demon Fire

Most colonial towns had a constable positioned as the chief law enforcement agent, and Haniford was no different, although a need for one had rarely presented itself until Pastor Sinclair wrote his laws. Constable Eli Matthews held the position for several years after his initial election by the elders of the community. The pastor supported the selection and had subsequently molded and guided Eli into a second pair of eyes to help him look for anyone who might stray from his teachings. The pastor wrote the laws and judged the offenses, but the actual arrests filtered through the constable's office which gave the procedure a sense of fairness and accountability. In practice though, the pastor would always decide which infractions had occurred and who would be arrested along with which sentences would be handed down.

The trip to the Matthew's residence turned out to be excruciatingly long for David. His young legs could have run the entire way, but Cyrus' age prevented speedy travels, and there was no horse available to ride. David's main concern focused on the wellbeing of his mother, and although he was confident she had gotten away from the church, he did not have as much confidence in her remaining hidden for long.

They passed the church during the trip, but nothing seemed out of place. There was no sign of movement in or around the area. David did not know whether that was a good omen or not, but he did not dwell on the question. His focus stayed on the task at hand which was to meet with the constable, and the more he thought about the situation the more he felt that his story would be accepted. He was not the only witness to the crime. His mother's account would be the same, and although being a woman placed her a few rungs lower on the societal ladder, both of their testimonies together would give the pastor no choice but to admit his transgressions. Her bloodied mouth and ripped cloths along with his busted hand would lead credence to their story as well.

David's positive outlook wavered, however, as he and Cyrus turned a corner and Constable Matthew's house came into view. To the left of the residence tied to the hitching post stood Pastor Sinclair's horse. "He's here." David stated.

Demon Fire

"Yes, it seems like the pastor has arrived before us." Cyrus acknowledged as he looked over and saw the concerned look on David's face. "Do not fear son. We will speak to the constable."

The pair walked up on the porch and knocked. "Come in!" Yelled a voice from inside, and Cyrus opened the door. The front room of the house was set up as office space for the constable. A desk sat centered in the room along with matching bookshelves to either side. The area had been arranged to hold work related meetings and appointments without interference to the living spaces.

At the desk sat Constable Matthews in an old wore down chair, and in a seat next to him was Pastor Sinclair holding a rag to his nose. The pastor spoke first, and although his voice had a nasally ring, he still had command of his speech which never failed to impress those within ear range. He talked in a calm authoritative manner which seemed uncanny to David considering the situation. "Come Cyrus. Have a seat." He said with a motion of his hand to a chair opposite his. "David, you sit over there next to the wall." David looked over at the small chair off to the side.

"I think I will stand if that's okay with you pastor." The hate-filled tension in his voice was noticed by everyone present.

At this point Constable Matthews spoke in a loud tone. "David, you will sit in that chair. You will speak when you are told to speak, and you will show respect to Pastor Sinclair and to this office! Do I make myself clear on that?"

"Yes sir." David said as he slunk into his seat. Despite the emotions of the night, he still knew his place. He needed the constable's assistance and showing disrespect would not help the situation.

"Now let's get down to the matter at hand." It was clear that the constable would take the lead during this impromptu meeting. "Mr. Cyrus, I am thankful to you for bringing young David here. It saves me the trouble of going out and looking for him." Constable Matthews turned to where David was sitting uncomfortably. "And David, I thank you for coming voluntarily to answer these charges."

"You're welcome." David said, not really understanding what the constable was talking about.

Cyrus spoke up. "Forgive me for interrupting constable, but I am confused. You spoke of answering charges. I have talked at length with David, and from what I am to understand, there should be no charges for him to answer. Quite the opposite; as in fact he has levied accusations himself against the pastor for which we have come here seeking council."

"Preposterous!" Pastor Sinclair exclaimed as he exited the chair and faced his adversary. "What possible accusations could you bring against me? The most serious infraction this community has ever seen has just taken place.

I have tried to keep calm, but I cannot fathom this mere boy sitting here before me being so obtuse as to think he might speak an utterance of negativity!"

Cyrus was taken aback by the outburst as David was rendered speechless. He was still uncertain about what everyone was talking about, but Cyrus understood completely.

"Pastor Sinclair. With all due respect I feel I deserve an explanation here. I have heard a very disturbing statement about goings on today, and if there is another side to the story, I would like to hear it."

"Constable Matthews I give the floor back to you." The pastor said. "This is not the time or the place for details, but a list of the charges is public knowledge, and Cyrus being a distinguished member of society has a right to know."

After standing, Constable Matthews picked up two pieces of parchment paper. An abundant amount of useful writing paper was not available so its use had been limited to important items that must be documented such as the written laws and legal letters designating land or property rights. "These papers Mr. Cyrus are the beginnings of two arrest warrants that will be filled out today. The first warrant has the name David Devlin attached."

Cyrus' confusion was clear to all. The story he had been told previously did not prepare him for this scenario. Being a man in control of his thoughts and feelings did not lend itself well to a situation where he was made to question long-held beliefs. David had been unsure himself, but the last sentence spoken was clear as day, and his face beamed red as he rose to protest. The constable had expected the animosity and had grasped the re-purposed chair leg he kept under the desk for just such an occasion, and before David was erect from his seated position, he came face to face with the working end of the makeshift club.

As the stick fluttered an inch or two up and down Constable Matthews spoke in a stern voice, but low enough that Cyrus and the pastor barely heard. "I warned you before there will be nothing but respect from you while dealing with this office. This can't be a surprise since you understand perfectly well what you have done - but then again, I don't really care if you understand it or not. All I know is what you have been accused of, and I know there is a warrant describing some despicable charges with your name on it. Most importantly though, I know that if you do not sit back down in that chair right now, and do exactly as I say we will forgo the trial and the sentencing, and I will bash your brains out right here on this floor."

Cyrus could not believe the words the constable spoke. He could imagine nothing that David might have done that would be horrible enough to cause this much emotion to emanate from the constable, but he did know things were getting out of control, and he thought there was a need to settle the emotions down before someone got hurt.

"Gentlemen please!" Cyrus spoke toward David and the constable. Pastor Sinclair had not moved from his seat during the confrontation. "David, sit down in your chair!"

"But Mr. Cyrus you…"

"David now is not the time for this. You must sit down. Mr. Matthews is the town's constable, and he is in charge of this situation. Right or wrong, you have to trust in the process and let calmer heads prevail. If there are formal charges present against you, then there is no choice but to submit. Be assured that you will have your say in the matter. There is a procedure that should be adhered to. Constable Matthews has obviously listened to Pastor Sinclair's side of the story, and he needs to hear yours as well, but it will be on his terms. For now remain calm and please take a seat in your chair."

David eased back down keeping his eye on the constable as he did so. As the chair creaked with acknowledgement of the weight, Constable Matthews moved back to his desk.

"Would a reading of the charges be appropriate?" Cyrus was interested to find out what all the fuss was about. David's story had been inflammatory, but obviously the other side had a different take on events. Following a nod of approval from the pastor, the constable read from the paper.

Chris Cumbie

"In the name of the Office of Constable written at the Town of Haniford on this twenty-second day of May, it has been sworn to me by a distinguished and outstanding member of our community whose image and word is impeccable in both poise and dignity that the following has truthfully occurred this very day. David Devlin and his mother Rachel Devlin were seen by the eye of a witness to have been in the act of unholy relations with one another. The act of carnal knowledge having transpired between the two…"

David had been listening intently to the words that emanated from the constable's mouth until the point when the blow landed. Now as his eyes opened, he realized that he was lying prone on a dirt floor. His face was pressed into the ground by the weight of his body which must have fallen down into a clump. It was dark, and he was alone, but in his current situation little else could be determined about his condition or location. He decided that his best course of action would be to move into a more comfortable position and then determine how to proceed after that. As his head lifted and turned, however, the pain rushed in with a vengeance. His eyes fluttered and consciousness left him once more.

Demon Fire

Pastor Sinclair took charge as David lay on the floor of the constable's Office bleeding from his head wound. "Constable, tell your helper Joseph to bring a horse around to the side door. We will be out soon." As the constable left the room, the pastor turned to Cyrus "You can plainly see the anger in this young man Cyrus. He cannot control his emotions, and I will tell you why. Constable Matthews was trying to explain to you and David both by reading the charges, but I will skip the formalities and lay it out for you instead. Rachel had asked me last Sunday if it would be possible to have a private counseling session with her and her son at their house instead of at my study. She said there were some serious issues that needed to be brought to light. I told her that would not be a problem. I do many home visits especially with the sick and elderly. I advised that it would be Wednesday before I could arrive, but by Tuesday I had caught up with my lessons and ventured out to their place. The two of them had obviously not expected my arrival. As I stepped up onto the porch I heard rustling noises from the inside, then a loud bang as if something crashed against the floor. I opened the door to check on things and I saw the most unholy act imaginable. I still cannot banish the sight from my mind."

The emotion emanating from the pastor was a thing of beauty. His talent at manipulation was in full force, and

Cyrus was none the wiser. As the story ended the constable and Joseph entered the room. Cyrus wore a look of uncertainty while he tried to process the information that had just been received, but it was too horrible and too out of the ordinary for him to wrap his head around it. The thought of a mother and son laying together in that way appalled him. Of course he had heard the recollection of David, but the way in which the pastor presented his argument was difficult to ignore. The only real evidence, other than the spoken words of the two, was David's hand and the pastor's face. Although the nose had clotted and the speaking ability had not been hampered, it was easy to see that the pastor had been hit and David was obviously the one who committed the battery. Cyrus had seen the anger first hand from the young man not five minutes ago. Anybody could tell by looking into David's eyes, before the blow from the stick, that he was about to harm the constable. No matter who was right and who was wrong Cyrus made a determination to trust in the system. He assumed that constable Matthews would not jump to conclusions, and that a fair process would occur to settle the issue.

"Let's get David into confinement." The pastor suggested with nodding approval from all, including Cyrus.

Once outside, the pastor mounted his horse as David's limp body hung over another. The procession then left for the church. Upon arrival David was dragged into the empty shack out back and thrown to the floor of the makeshift cell where his body settled in a mass. Joseph set a bowl of water to the side as he shut and locked the large wooden doors. Cyrus told the group at that point he was going back home. The day had been brutal to his senses, and a nap was long overdue. Pastor Sinclair thanked him for bringing David in and wished him well on his way with a reminder that he might be called on for a hearing to deal with the Devlin situation. Cyrus promised he would remain available as he headed back down the road toward home.

After running from the church, Rachel headed into the woods and found an old trail she used to hike as a young girl. She ran for a while and then transitioned to a quick walk once she felt she had made it a safe distance away. When she slowed her pace the emotions of what had just occurred tried to overtake her. She stopped cold in her tracks and forced the thoughts deep into the back of her mind and steadied her resolve. She told herself that David had to be her main concern. His barging into the room had saved a terrible thing from happening, and for that she was grateful, but now his life was in danger because of it. There was little doubt in her mind that the pastor would have killed David with the knife if he had been able to reach further with his outstretched arm. If a person attempted what the pastor had tried to do to her, then that person would be capable of doing anything.

    Rachel took a moment to ponder the options. She had to find David, but the way to go about doing that was not readily known. First she had no idea where he would end up. There was no doubt that his legs were capable of carrying him far away from the pastor's grasp, but he could not run forever. It was possible that he traveled to the safety of the woods like she did. Along with a talent for working the fields, David was adept at surviving off of nature. He could stay hidden for long periods of time if need be. He might also come looking for her or try to find help in the community somehow. All of these options left her confused as to what to do next. After weighing all the pros and cons, she headed home. She knew it would be a risk, but once inside the house she could lock the doors and arm herself against the pastor if he looked for her there. It was possible that her son would choose the same course of action and they would reunite there.

    The trip home was uneventful. Plenty of trails meandered through the area, and she used them to stay hidden from view as she went. There were a few places where the main road crossed, but no other travelers passed her way. She avoided all the houses since she did not know who could be trusted or where her tormentor might be, and the fact that he was the most important and powerful man in the community weighed heavily on her. The story she had to tell would not be readily accepted, and even with her son's account to bolster it, most people would think it was only a made up lie.

The trail leading to her house traversed a ridge just to the south. From this vantage point Rachel could see the landscape below and here she would remain for a short time to make sure no one was around. As she sat on a boulder to survey the area below and rest her tired legs, she contemplated the happenings of the day. Her entire world seemed to have turned upside down in an instant. She had suffered through tragedy before, and she understood the ability to overcome this was within her, but it would not be easy. The belief in her community and especially in her pastor had never wavered, and she had been content in the life that had been provided for her and her son; but now everything she knew and trusted had changed.

After an hour passed her confidence that no one was in or around the house increased to the point that she made her way down. That the house lay empty was both a relief and a concern. She was glad that the danger from the pastor did not precede her, but the hope that David might have returned home to meet her vanquished. Rachel completed the journey home and locked the door once inside the residence. She made something to eat keeping an eye on the window, and when finished she took a large butcher knife with her to a chair and tried to relax. Using knives was not uncommon to her since frequently she had been called upon to portion meat out for future consumption. Rachel had hoped not to have to wield the tool as a weapon, but she knew in her heart that if Pastor Sinclair walked through the door, the blade would lay his neck wide.

The knock came again, this time with more persistence. Rachel rose from her seat and steadied herself. She did not know how long she had been asleep in the chair, but it must have been hours. She immediately picked up the knife which had fallen from her grasp as slumber arrived. She took her first step toward the door as a voice shouted from the other side.

"Rachel, this is Constable Matthews! Open up!"

Rachel froze in place. She had assumed Pastor Sinclair or maybe David would be at her door. The constable visiting had not been an option she had considered. A sense of relief crept into her thoughts until she realized that he might not be alone.

"I am here constable. Who is there with you?"

"Only myself and Joseph. We have important business to speak with you about so open the door."

Rachel went to the counter and laid the knife down. She had no reason to fear anyone but the pastor. As she opened the door Constable Matthews spoke again.

"Hello Rachel. I'm sorry I must visit you under these circumstances, but I need you to come with us back to my office. There have been accusations made against you and David that must be answered."

"Accusations?" Rachel's confusion showed on her face as she spoke loudly. "What accusations could have possibly been made against us?"

"I would rather talk about this at the office. This is not the conversation to have standing on one's front porch. I will explain everything in time. I have horses at the end of the drive awaiting us. You would do well not to question me on this matter."

She did not question him further. Rachel actually felt safe in the constable's care, and a sense of duty to obey a duly elected law enforcement officer compelled her to follow his direction. She did not think David would be at the house anytime soon anyway. She believed he would stay hidden for the time being, and she was more than confident that he could fend for himself. The sun was setting in the distance as she gathered her coat and mounted one of the horses waiting outside. She rode with Joseph while Constable Matthews followed close behind on his own steed. During the ride back into town Rachel contemplated how she would approach talking to the constable about what happened at the church. She thought someone should hear about what took place, and who better than him. Maybe he could help her figure out what to do about the pastor. She was not sure what he meant by accusations, but she believed her questions would be answered once they arrived at the office. A bit of confidence crept up, and she thought everything might be okay after all.

David awoke for the second time gasping for air. The sudden blast of cold water jerked him awake as his nose and mouth suddenly filled with liquid. Coughing and spitting he turned to his side while a sharp pain ran through the entire length of his body. As the spasms calmed, he was able to take a solid breath and lift a hand to his head. A good deal of swelling had occurred, and it was painful to the touch. He let out a groan as a voice spoke behind him.

"I never understood why the constable kept a broken chair leg next to his desk before. I always thought it a strange aesthetic, but I guess we now know what its true purpose was."

David spun around as fast as his damaged head would let him. He recognized the voice, having listened to it every Sunday since he could remember. Hearing it now sent a shiver down his spine, and he realized where the water had originated from. Pastor Sinclair still held the empty wooden bucket in his hand as he spoke.

"I do apologize David. This unfortunate set of events has turned out to be a distraction for us. You of course were not supposed to be in this predicament, but alas some things just have a way of working out in ways we might not plan. So that leaves us with an obstacle to overcome. You are in a weakened state at the moment. There is a pretty good gash to your head that has swollen nicely, and the pain has made you weak. In your current condition you are no threat, but unfortunately for you it is a temporary state. I have no doubt that you will gain strength back quickly and then young David, I assume that you will try to kill me." The pastor paused for greater effect after the last statement.

"Now do not misunderstand me." The pastor began again. "I hold no grudge toward you for the animosity. You have perceived a wrong that has occurred, and you expect retribution for it. I can sympathize completely. I in fact would feel the same way were the circumstances reversed. But as the fates would have it circumstances are not reversed. I am too important in this community to suffer any negative outcome from this David. I think you know this to be the case. You have a story that you are trying to convince someone to accept. The problem for you is that I have a story of my own to tell. Mine is a story unlike yours, however. Mine is a story people want to believe, it is a story people need to believe, and trust me when I tell you this. It is a story people will believe."

David could not bring himself to respond. The pastor was an evil person willing to spread lies and ruin lives to keep any semblance of wrongdoing from sullying his pristine image. He had manipulated the entire community into thinking his only purpose in life was to serve them and to care for their needs. David realized that every moment from the time the pastor rode into town on his magnificent horse until now, had been false, including the stories that had he told of travels and adventures to lands near and far. At this point David even questioned the validity of the church that the pastor led. He could no longer tolerate a religious foundation that had produced a leader such as this.

David's heart turned cold. The chances of him and his mother turning the community against the pastor were non-existent. There was but one avenue for the revenge he felt was deserved and that was just as the pastor had assumed. He must take the life of this monster that stood before him. Not only take his life, but take away the very tool he had used to overpower the people of Haniford. So that became the plan. There were details to hash out, but as soon as possible the pastor would be dead and the church would be destroyed.

"There it is." The pastor spoke as he looked down menacingly at David. "There is the look I knew would come. Yesterday you were a great young man with plenty of promise. You worked hard, you studied the Bible lessons, you cared for others. How quickly you have changed into a hardened killer." The pastor laughed out loud at this last statement. "Tell me then. How will you proceed? Build up your strength maybe? Hide behind the door and await my arrival? Hit me over the head? Convince Joseph to bring you a knife for some silly reason? Just how do you plan on killing me David?" There was laughter again before a slight pause. "I see murder in your eyes, but what I don't see is much intelligence. You are busy making plans in your mind and you never even finished listening to the charges brought against you before you were not so gently shown the floor."

"Your young strong frame could easily end my life once you regain strength, and since I cannot let that happen I must find a way to end your life first. You, of course, are charged with striking another without provocation. My nose, and your hand will attest to that fact, but that is of little concern to either of us because a minor charge such as that would serve no one's interests to pursue. Heresy my boy, heresy is the charge we will focus on, and it is the charge you will be convicted of and sentenced to die for."

"How in the world are you are going to convict me of that?" David had found a touch of energy through his anger, and the statement was louder and more pronounced that either of them had thought possible under the circumstances. "I have done nothing wrong. You are the one who has committed a crime, and I might not have the ability to prove it, but what could you ever prove against me?" As he spoke David's chest lifted, and he was almost sitting straight up on the dirt floor.

The pastor gripped the water bucket tight. He did not assume that David had the energy to put up much of a fight, but he figured a swift blow might be in order if he was wrong.

"Well, since you asked." The pastor's voice took a sarcastic tone as he shifted position to bring him a step or two closer. "Let me explain something to you. You ask how I will prove the charges. The fact is that I will not try to prove anything at all nor will I need to. Your admission of guilt will be proof enough for everyone involved."

The bewilderment present on David's face amused the pastor. "I see you are puzzled. You recall the constable had two warrants in his hand do you not?"

David tried to remember the meeting in the constable's Office, but most of it was a blur at the moment.

"One warrant of course was for you. The second was for your mother, and the charges of heresy stem from the fact that I found the two of you having carnal relations with each other."

David's face turned red as he struggled to his feet. This atrocious statement would not be tolerated. The bucket was raised in defense, but there was no need for it to fall since David's first step in the direction of the pastor found him back on the floor. His love for Rachel was unquestionable, and the suffering he was enduring was nothing compared to the thought of the pastor involving his mother in whatever evil scheme he was concocting.

"I understand your concern for her. She is a precious woman, and I, like you, would hate for her to suffer any hardship from this situation. However, her charge happens to be the same as yours. There is no need to dwell on the details, just realize where you are now and where she could end up. A conviction of the crime, as you remember from your lessons, is punishable by death, and believe me when I tell you that both of you will be convicted. There is no doubt about that. I have already written papers. A hearing is all that is necessary for it to be official, and who do you think will be in attendance at that hearing? Yes, the same people that have determined your fate so far this day. Do you understand what I am saying?"

David had rolled back to a seated position and stared at the pastor with a defeated look on his face. No words of argument came. He knew everything that had been said would more than likely occur. He was not delusional enough to believe someone would come to his aid. Even Cyrus was of no help to him now. David was not fearful of death or persecution, and he was not afraid of standing up to anyone or anything, but his wellbeing was not the only thing to consider. His mother would perish along with him if the scenario played out the way the pastor had proposed, and David would not let that happen. All he could do to save her would be done.

"What would you have me do?" David asked with total dejection emanating from his voice.

"You will plead guilty to all charges brought against you while retracting all accusations made against me. You shall admit to each charge independently and take the blame as the instigator of the incident. Part of your admission will be that you forced yourself on your mother. If she is an unwilling victim, then she can be absolved of any wrongdoing. You will admit these facts in front of me, Constable Matthews and a witness of my choosing. You will then be put to death by fire as per the heresy law. You will do this without hesitation or malice toward me or the process in general, and in doing so you will save your mother from the same fate. I will discard her warrant and declare her a free woman."

David responded almost in a whisper. "How do I know that you won't try and hurt her again?

"I understand the regard you have for your mother. I could give you my word that no harm would come to her, but I am sure that would be of no consequence to you. The fact is that there is no way for me to assure you she will remain safe. I can promise, however, that if my directions are not followed then she will follow you into the flames."

Chris Cumbie

Chapter 10
Outside the Box

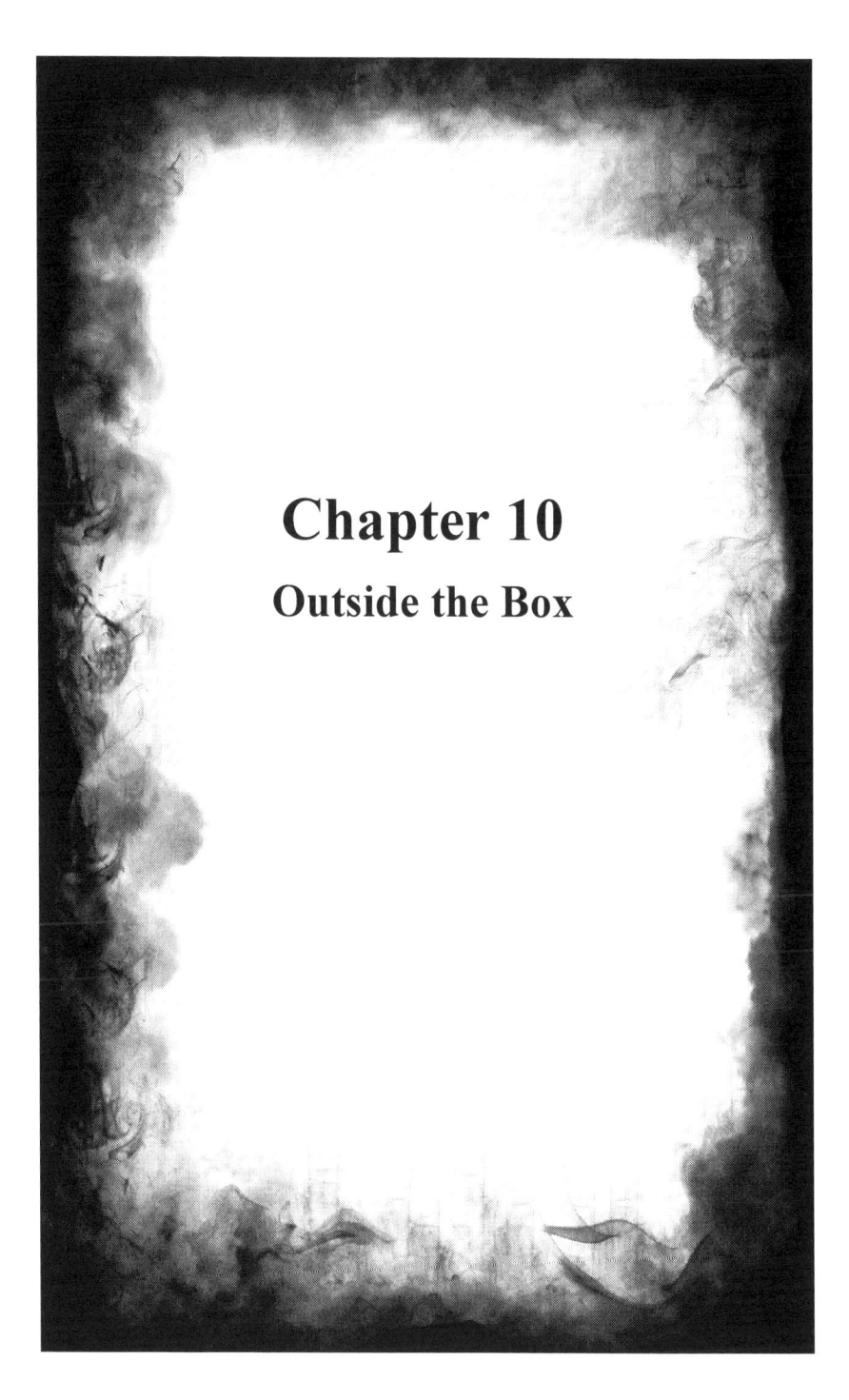

Chris Cumbie

"Hey Sarah. What's up?"

"I finished up at the church. Do you have a minute to talk?"

"Yeah, I'm just in the office finishing up paperwork." Jake said.

"Well, the entry point was a side door that had a window busted out by a rock, and there are points of origin all over the place. Pastor Stephens was there when the fire started, but he didn't see anyone or anything, and there were no other witnesses. All the firefighters spoke about how strange the fire acted, just like I figured they would. Oh, and one other thing. You know the gas torch your department uses at the training center?"

"Yeah. I'm familiar with it." Jake answered.

"Well, it's here."

"It's there at the church?"

"Yep. It was sitting inside. I assume Terry brought it with him."

"Okay, Sarah this is getting to be too much." Jake was not trying to hide his annoyance at the situation. "So you are telling me Terry left the station, picked up the torch, went to the church, set it on fire and remembers none of it? This is just not possible."

"I know. It sounds impossible to me too, but we are trained to look at the facts, and the facts say that what you just described is what happened."

There was a pause as Jake took a moment to process what he had heard.

"Okay. So what do you suggest we do now?" Jake asked.

"Here's the thing." Sarah began. "You remember that Detective Maxwell talked about all the strange occurrences he has come across. He knows what we are dealing with is out of the ordinary, and his suggestion was to think outside of the box and to take a break from our logic. So you asked what I think. I think exactly that. We need to come at this from a different perspective. With all the strangeness of these fires maybe we should go talk with someone that is a little strange. What do you think?" Sarah was not sure if Jake would be on board with her idea. She felt like her outlook on life was a little more progressive than his, and even she felt that this line of thinking sounded too weird to take seriously.

"Well crap Sarah. I don't have any better suggestions. Where do you think we should begin?"

Sarah felt more at ease. If she was going to take a walk on the crazy side, at least she wouldn't be alone.

"I've already started. I got off the phone with Detective Maxwell just before I called you, and he gave me the name of someone local to talk to. You aren't going to believe who it is either."

"Who?" Jake asked.

"Charlie Brinkman."

"Really? He thinks we should talk to Charlie Brinkman? What the heck is Charlie going to tell us other than when the next superhero movie is coming out?"

"I know, I know. He wouldn't be my first choice as a resource, but we are supposed to be thinking outside of the box here remember?"

"Yeah, I suppose you are right. But Charlie? Good lord." Jake was laughing by the time he spoke the last sentence. Everyone always loved Charlie, or Chuck or Charles or any number of names depending on who one was talking to. They loved him in spite of, and sometimes because of, his awkwardly high-energy personality. Jake and Charlie had attended the same school, but Jake was a few years older. Sarah had known him as well and she was fond of his quirky nature although her skepticism of his help in this matter remained high. Jake reluctantly agreed to set up a meeting and promised to update her.

Charlie had traveled out of state to attend college on an academic scholarship. Everyone in the community had been proud when he graduated at the top of his class, but very few, including Jake, understood why he came back to town to open a comic book store. Charlie was at the store when Jake called. He had not eaten lunch so an offer to bring over Chinese food was made and accepted.

Jake actually looked forward to the meeting. First, he loved the Lo Mein noodles from the Yuncheng Garden Buffet. Second, since he did not think the meeting would lead to anything productive, Jake thought it might be a good opportunity to relax and catch up with an old friend, and maybe even forget about all the stress for an hour or so.

The comic book store was on the far west side of Deer Creek in the town of Thomasville Flats. The population hovered around 15,000 which would not seem substantial enough to support a business as expansive as Charlie's. Nearly 12,000 square feet of space made up the building and it spread out over two stories. The street level included the retail space, a reading area, and a large gaming room that included board and virtual reality games. There was a loft style living area upstairs where Charlie stayed, but that was not enough to fill the entire area. It was assumed that the extra space had been used for storage, but no one knew for certain, and no one really cared that much either.

Jake entered the store and marveled at the seemingly never ending shelves of comics and collectibles. There were three teens in the back playing a board game and one customer perusing the isles as a young clerk played on her phone behind the counter. Charlie exited the office area as Jake entered and the door chime rang.

"Hey Jake, how are you doing man." Charlie was almost speed-walking across the floor to shake hands. "It's been a while since we've seen each other. You are looking fit." Jake was smiling and nodding although he couldn't find an opening to say anything. Charlie was a talkative fellow, and he was great at complimenting people. Making people feel good made him feel equally so. Charlie had a youthful look to him that made those looking to stop their own aging processes envious. His curly head of hair and stunningly light blue eyes made the girls swoon, although to Charlie's dismay it was usually the younger high school girls that looked his way instead of someone his own age – someone that he might actually be interested in pursuing.

After a quick bro-hug, Charlie motioned for Jake to follow. "Let's head back to my office. There's a table where we can spread this food out." After stopping by the vending machine for drinks, the two settled in for lunch. The room was large and extremely cluttered. Antique movie posters decorated the walls, along with his college diploma, and stacks of forms and books piled up on the desk and bookshelves. Jake assumed that the appearance of disorganization was misleading. He knew Charlie was well organized and had what many people thought was an eidetic memory. More than likely there was not a single piece of paper, form, or post-it-note in the entire building he did not know both the exact location and the information it contained.

As they sat and ate, stories flowed back and forth about topics ranging from high school escapades to college life. Jake was enjoying his time with Charlie and for a while he forgot the reason for stopping by. It was the first time since answering the call about the cabin fire that he had taken a breath and relaxed. Although the respite was appreciated, it was short lived as Charlie followed a brief pause in the conversation with the question they were both expecting.

"So what brings you to my humble establishment? I'm assuming it's not to bolster your comic collection."

Jake sighed as his head tilted down. "Yeah, I guess we need to get to the topic at hand. I am not here on a social call Charlie. There is a case I am working that has got me stumped."

"Is it the cabin fire? I heard about the fire chief and his son. That was a horrible tragedy."

"It was a heartbreaking situation for all of us, but I'm here more about two fires that have occurred since then." Jake said. "Actually, to tell the truth, I don't really know why I am here. No offense, but what possible advice you could give me about these investigations is beyond me."

"Well let's not jump to conclusions yet. You are correct in assuming I'm not well versed in arson investigations, but there is a reason you are here so why don't we back up and go from there. I would be more than happy to help you in any way possible Jake so let's see what we've got."

"I guess it's worth a shot." Jake appreciated someone at least wanting to help, and since he was already there, he figured that it would not hurt to at least talk it out. Maybe someone from the outside hearing the situation might bring some new insight.

"Okay great. So let's begin with that initial question. What brought you to my threshold?"

Jake relaxed a little more as he continued to speak. "I think it was a combination of Detective Maxwell and Sarah. You know Detective Maxwell don't you?"

"I am familiar with him, and you bringing his name up is enlightening. So what about Sarah?"

"Sarah is working the case with me. One of the church fires is in her jurisdiction, but she has run into the same roadblocks I have. She is the one that spoke with the detective and convinced me to come see you. What do you mean by enlightening?"

"Ah. Well I have advised the good detective on cases in the past. Only a few times since he is a more than capable investigator, but when there is a particular case that has, as you say gotten him stumped, he will call on my services."

Jake looked around the room at the movie posters and the cluttered desk with his gaze coming to rest on the grin-filled face of Charlie, and he regretted his next statement the moment the harsh words left his mouth.

"What the heck kind of advice could you give about an investigation to Detective Maxwell?" Jake tried to backtrack as soon as he spoke. "Look I didn't mean that."

"It's okay Jake. You have been under a lot of stress, and it would seem strange to anyone looking from the outside in that a nerdy comic book guy could possibly help an experienced world traveling detective, but not everything is always as it seems. Our minds are programmed to function in stereotypical fashion. Our reality is corrupted by what we have always known, and when something unusual occurs we find ways to make the scenario fit nicely into our boxes of knowledge."

Jake was impressed with the way Charlie could transition from his awkwardly friendly style to the straight laced seriousness he exhibited now.

Demon Fire

"The problem is that not everything in this world fits into our normal way of thinking. That's where my services come into play. I have a certain way of looking past the practical aspects of life that comes in handy from time to time. That being said, I am contacted on occasion by various people who need a different viewpoint. Detective Maxwell has been one of those people in the past. Now that we have that out of the way, why don't we get to the reason for your visit today? So am I correct in assuming these fires contain something strange or unexplained about them?"

"That is a bit of an understatement." Jake said. "I have never seen or heard of anything like these two church fires before, but I've got to tell you Charlie. I'm not sure what help you will be. I mean no offense, but I'm skeptical. I kind of enjoy living in my normal reality."

"That's fine Jake. Trust me. There are very few people that sit across from me in these instances with anything other than cynicism. I will ask you what I ask them. What do you have to lose? Usually if I'm involved, all options have been exhausted. There are no leads, and no other resources available to tap into. So if this describes you then there are two options. Go back to figuring out things that make no sense or work with me. Give me a few details and see where it gets us. A different view can't hurt even if it is a whacked out way of thinking."

"Okay Charlie. I guess you're right. It can't hurt, and restating the events might just spark a new theory in my brain."

"That a boy. Now start from the beginning. Tell me the details and focus on the oddities since I'm sure you have figured out all the normal stuff by now."

"Well, as I said, there have been two church fires. The first was at the Life of God Church right here in Deer Creek. Chief Taylor was there, and he was actually the one that called 911. All the evidence I gathered shows that the fire was intentionally set, and everything points to the chief as being the one who started it. The second fire occurred the next morning at the First Christian Church of Newton. A firefighter with our department named Terry Wade was at the scene when the fire occurred, and all the evidence points to him starting that fire. Both Chief Taylor and Firefighter Wade claim they had blacked out during the time of the fires and that they did not coordinate with each other, which would be laughable except for the fact that they both aced polygraph tests."

"Well that is interesting, and it is a strange aspect to the story. What else?" Charlie asked.

"The firefighters on both scenes reported strange occurrences with the fires themselves. The flames were described as shooting out in various directions with seemingly no outside forces acting upon them. I know that it might seem that flames will go in different directions naturally, but there are certain physical laws that are constant, and according to some senior firefighters those laws were broken with these two fires. That is about all the information available. Both Firefighter Wade and Chief Taylor are in jail without bond. Even though their stories about blacking out and not knowing what happened seem to be true, there is still plenty of evidence that they are the ones that started the fires."

"Okay. That gives us a starting point to work from." Charlie said. "And nothing in your investigation answers any of these oddities correct?"

"That is right. Sarah is working with me, and neither one of us have any idea on how to answer these questions. This is nothing that either of us has dealt with before."

"Ah Sarah. She's a great gal Jake. Have you and her gotten back together yet?"

"No, we are not together Charlie. You ask that question like our getting back together is inevitable."

"Well, it should be a foregone conclusion. You and Sarah were made for each other. It has always seemed that you two are the only ones that aren't able to see that."

"If you say so." Jake was not in the mood to discuss his love life at the moment. Restating the confusing facts of the cases only made him unsure if they would ever be solved.

"Alright, so I think I can help." Charlie's voice raised an octave as he spoke. He seemed to get excited about the prospect of helping with Jake's investigations. "The first step is to get you to trust in me and the process. We are going out on a limb together and I need you all the way out on the edge with me. Do you think you can do that Jake?"

Jake was far from certain, but he gave assurances that he would try.

"That's good enough for me." Charlie said. "Now, I will assume the subjects were burned at the fires?"

"Yes." Jake confirmed. "They were both burned, but how did you guess that?"

"I didn't know for certain, but the scenario you laid out sounds familiar."

"It sounds familiar?" Jake was puzzled and his skepticism could not be hidden from his question.

"Yes indeed. Not the same details of course, but the same general facts no doubt. I assume you aren't buying what I am saying Jake. Let's go upstairs, and maybe you will understand a little better.

Jake agreed and as they exited the office, the clerk was given a few instructions about inventory and they proceeded to a set of stairs at the far end of the hallway. As the door opened onto the second floor, Jake was amazed at the open loft space that had been converted into Charlie's apartment. High end furniture and appliances filled the space along with an elaborate gaming and entertainment center. Jake had questioned how such a large comic book shop could sustain itself in a small community, and with the large amount of money that had been put into the living space, he questioned it even more now.

Seeing the look on Jake's face, Charlie responded. "All of your questions will be answered soon."

Windows surrounded three sides of the space with the fourth being a solid wall splitting the second floor into equal parts. The two made their way to a solid steel door in the center of the wall. The door was substantial, supposedly for security purposes, but it opened with little effort as the keypad lock was ignored.

Jake's jaw dropped as his eyes adjusted to the subdued lighting and he was exposed to the area behind the door. The open space seemed to have three separate sections. The section to his right held floor-to-ceiling bookshelves. The shelves themselves were curved with a dark brown exterior which made for a winding walk down the aisle and to Jake's mind worked quite well within the space. In the center of the room was a long conference style table with piles of books and papers stacked on top. There were two fine leather chairs that matched the deep tones of the wooden table top and the bookshelves. On the far side of the table Jake noticed glass enclosed display stands containing what looked like antique books and manuscripts.

The most impressive part of the impromptu tour was on the left side of the room, however. Rows of computer towers lined the walls with a large console comprising a myriad of computer terminals placed in a semi circle around a center chair. The whole scene looked like it could have been pulled straight out of a science fiction film.

"What the heck is all this?" Jake asked when he was able to collect himself.

"This, my friend, is information. As you probably figured out by now, selling comic books is my hobby. Information gathering, sorting and disseminating is my profession, and something I get reimbursed well for as you can see." Charlie did not seem to brag. To Jake it felt more like an educational talk than anything else, and an education he was obviously not the first to partake in. "Come Jake. Let's take a seat, and I will try to explain." The two sat in the conference table chairs as Charlie brightened the lights slightly and continued. "Let me first tell you how I got to be an information guy. I know that is not a very impressive title, but it is what I do and who I am. It began in college and not because of anything I did. I never would have imagined, although it seems logical now, that the upper echelon of universities are watched rather closely. Certain professors, fellow students, the occasional visitor posing as a job hunter, all of these people are watching. Watching and recruiting. Looking for the perfect subject to mold and grow for their purposes. All types of organizations take part. The government of this country, of other countries, private corporations, law firms, they all do it, and although it sounds rather sinister, the practice is quite normal. Most of the recruiters are looking for good people to do good things. Now there are some that have nefarious goals, but that is unusual from what I have gathered since then."

"In my case, a benefactor was looking for a sponge. Someone that could handle large quantities of information from multiple sources and find the tidbits of knowledge needed. I never even knew I would be good at this kind of thing, but someone there saw something, and I was contacted. I left school early, yes the diploma on the wall downstairs is a fake, and I traveled to several locations around the globe to hone my skills. Now you might wonder why I came back here."

"I'm wondering a lot of things Charlie, but please continue." Jake stated with an air of amazement and trepidation.

"I understand completely. Most of my clients become familiar with my work before I am contacted, but there are quite a few unfamiliar with the process; so the conversation I am having with you is not my first. Anyway, my occupation is as old as history itself. There has always been a need for information. In the not-too-distant past it would have been necessary for me to live in a large metropolitan area with good communications and vast libraries. Now I keep my small arsenal of books as you see and some older copies that are not available digitally, but the vast majority of data I need is right over there." Charlie pointed to the computer area. "I use a cluster super computer set up through those towers. It is constantly checking the web and using complex formulas, invented I assume by computer geniuses recruited just like I was. Once the information flags and filters what is needed, then I come into play. I peruse the data and make determinations on what information is relevant to a specific customer. With my natural talent, training, and experience I have become quite adept at this unusual job." Charlie flashed a quick grin at Jake. "That is a synopsis of my world. Now for the question-and-answer period."

"Where do I even begin Charlie? That is an outlandish tale. Aren't you worried for your safety dealing with this stuff? I mean you work out of a comic book shop. The door to this place isn't even locked."

"That's an excellent question, and I have an excellent answer. I'm not a spy." Another grin as Charlie spoke. "I said this is information. I never said it was secretive. All of this data comes from the public web. I don't go deep at all. There is nothing here that the general person on the street couldn't find if they only knew where to look and how to interlock the clues. Also, I pick my own customers. I stay away from the sketchy stuff, and even if I were involved in all of that crap, my job is a little too boring and under the radar for anyone to care that much about it."

"Okay. So who are your customers?" Jake asked.

"Lots of different people and organizations. Of course Detective Maxwell has used my services. Government departments such as Defense and State. Um, the FBI has called at times as well as Fortune 500 companies. Also a few friendly countries, and sometimes the unfriendly ones, but I politely decline those."

"Hmm. Well I must admit when I walked in the front door of your shop I was expecting a good meal and a good time catching up with an old friend. I was not expecting any of this." Jake looked around the room as he spoke. "It is impressive, and as difficult as it is to wrap my mind around it, I don't doubt your story. I do wonder though how you could help me though."

"Well let me show you then." Charlie almost leaped out of his seat as Jake followed him to the command chair. The computers sprang to life as they entered the area and Charlie sat down. His fingers began to fly over an oversized keyboard with characters that were foreign to Jake. "One thing that most people don't realize is that there is not much that is new in the world. Humans have been around long enough and in such great numbers that if someone sees something or hears something or even does something, it has probably happened before, multiple times even. That is why I said your story sounded familiar. My memory is one of the greatest assets I have when it comes to this work. As I search through the data, I tend to remember most of what I see, and I can retrieve it when the time comes, such as now." His fingers moved across the keys with tremendous speed as he spoke. "Now all I need to do is a file search. The search engine on here is another proprietary tool. Developed no doubt by another genius recruit. I really would love to find out one day how many of us there are. I'm sure the information is out there, and of course I would be the one to find it. The trick is to find someone to pay me for it though." Charlie laughed at this, and Jake laughed also, more at Charlie's reaction than to the joke itself.

"Okay, I have set the parameters." A search box appeared and Charlie typed in the words Demon Fire.

"What are you doing? What does that mean?" Jake asked.

"Oh. Yeah. This search program is a little more specific than the ones you are used to. It helps if you place the words in order of importance. I am sure we are dealing with a demon-like being that is somehow related to fire so placing the words, in this order, will get me better results than just assuming it's a fire demon which it very well could be." Charlie continued to click away at the keyboard as search results popped up on one of the side monitors.

Demon Fire

"No Charlie. I don't care about your search engine." Jake had a look of disgust on his face as he talked. "What I'm asking is why are you looking for that junk? Demons? Really? I'm an idiot. I was starting to believe this might lead to something. What a joke." Jake turned and walked toward the door. "This is a nice place you have here Charlie." He stopped and did a half turn back. "I'm sure you are making good money feeding this crap to whoever is buying, but I have wasted enough time. I need to get back to the office and try to figure out my next step."

Charlie had continued typing as Jake spoke. After the last statement the typing stopped. "Glover Point Kansas, Collinsville Rhode Island, Columbia Beach Florida just to name a few." He never turned from his monitors as he spoke.

"What?" Jake saw several of the computer monitors had information scrolling at a rapid pace.

"All towns across the country that have had similar occurrences to the ones you described. It was a quick search pattern so there should be more results if I was to dig deeper, and I didn't even look globally. Very interesting stuff here Jake. Wanna come take a look?

Jake had already taken two steps back toward Charlie's position. He stopped again and shook his head. Why was he playing along with this madness? When he looked back on this moment later he realized the reason he played along was that he had no other options. Two people he had sworn to serve with and protect at all costs were in jail, and the thought of turning down even the possibility of an answer was more than he could bear.

"Okay Charlie. Show me what you have found."

Chapter 11
Point of Origin

Chris Cumbie

Demon Fire

The confinement shack contained two makeshift cells, which would have left plenty of room for Rachel to accompany her son, although no one thought that would be a good idea. The pastor wanted no one providing alternate views on how he saw things playing out. Rachel could easily lead her son in directions that were contrary. Constable Matthews went along with the pastor's thinking, although he was not made aware of the motives. The solution was to have Rachel stay at the Matthew's house, so once the two horses and their burdens arrived she was led to a spare room in the attic. The room was not large enough for a bed, but there was a small cot against the far wall that would be suitable for sleep. Several wooden boxes were stacked in the corner, and save for a single shelf with a lantern on top, there was nothing else. A single door led to and from the room which locked from the outside with a key. The lone window looked out over the side yard, but neither the door nor window offered much in the way of hope for escape since the window could have been left open and the door unlocked, and it still would not change the fact that there was no place for her to go. Rachel had a home, and she had friends in the community, but Haniford was a close knit town loyal to the pastor, and it would not take long for someone to find her and bring her back to this same room.

There had been little detail given about the accusations although she knew an arrest warrant had been signed against her and David, and she assumed that he had been placed in the confinement shack. Rachel's only concern was for his safety. The Constable had assured her that he had not been mistreated, but she was unsure of anyone or anything now that her entire world had been thrown into chaos.

Gloria Matthews, the Constable's wife, made supper that night and when she and her husband were finished, she prepared a plate and took it to Rachel's room. Rachel was polite and thankful for the sustenance. All the worry from the day had dampened her appetite, but she made herself finish the entire plate. Little could be done under the circumstances, but keeping herself strong and alert was something she could control and something that might pay off if an advantageous situation presented itself.

Demon Fire

Rachel knew that no place existed for her to escape to. She had little knowledge of the world outside Haniford, and if she gained the ability to leave undetected, she would be at a loss with no friends available for support outside the confines of her known world. Besides, leaving David behind was not an option. Since his birth, he had been her entire reason for existing. The motherly instinct would prevent her from taking off even if she wanted to, so she would have to make do with the private little jail cell in the attic for the time being. Although making do did not mean she wouldn't venture out when it suited her needs. The window to the outside did not go unnoticed. Rachel keyed in on it the moment she walked into the room. She had always been strong and nimble so the trip through the window and down the side of the porch would be a breeze. The only concern would be someone seeing and stopping her, but she had to check on her son. Hearing he was doing okay would not be enough; she would have to see that fact personally.

After supper she waited until everyone retired to bed. Then she waited a little longer. Several hours passed until her level of comfort with leaving undetected had been reached. As she began the journey, she found that the window was not as easy as she had hoped to open. Several minutes of pushing and prying were necessary since she had to be careful of any noise. Keeping the Matthews from stirring was of greatest importance to realize her plan of visiting David. Finally, after much persistence, the window gave way. Rachel opened it wide and slipped out onto the roof of the porch below. The angle was not too steep, so she kept her feet under her while making her way to the corner and then gracefully shimmied down the support column. The walk to the church was uneventful since no one in town stirred at that time of night. Being hard workers made for a good night sleep for most everyone. Still, Rachel took care to stay out of the open as much as possible. She stayed close to the wood line so at a moment's notice she could slip unseen deep into the trees. As she approached the church, her pace slowed. Her thoughts traveled back to the incident that caused all of this madness. Before she realized it, the walk had ceased. Rachel stood still while staring at the building that had once given her so much calm and comfort and now held nothing for her but pain and sadness.

A noise from the back of the church snapped her back into an awareness of where she was and what she was doing. Fear took hold as she realized she was too far from the woods for immediate shelter, but standing out in the open did not make for a good option so she moved to the side of the building and hoped that whoever was out and about would not come her way. Another noise from the back and Rachel's fears were eased. There was a person visible, but they moved away from her and closer to the pastor's residence. Rachel quickly made her way to the adjacent corner, and as the next sound came, she felt comfortable enough to peak around to see Pastor Sinclair walking through the back door. He had been to the confinement shack but for what purpose she could not be sure. The shack usually stood unguarded even when occupied with a prisoner. The thickness of the wood and strength of the locks and latches prevented escape, and therefore the prisoners could be locked away with only sporadic checks necessary throughout the day.

Rachel decided that she would give the pastor time to settle. There was no way of knowing if he had turned in for the night or if he would be back, but after a short while she thought it safe enough to take a chance and move. The night was clear and quiet with her footfalls providing the only audible noise, which in her mind must have been loud enough to wake the dead. She made it to the outside wall of the building without detection though, and to her amazement the door to the inside of the shack was not locked. Once inside she understood why. In the far corner of the entry room leaning back in an old rickety chair sat the constable's helper, Joseph. Rachel's heart skipped a beat as she froze in place trying not to breathe. She was not so much in fear of her own safety, but she knew this might be her only chance to see David. If caught, she would more than likely find herself with a guard of her own and no way to escape again.

The seconds seemed like minutes as she stood as still as possible. Beads of sweat glistened down her cheek as she waited for movement. Joseph had been Constable Matthew's helper for the past couple of years, and he was competent at most chores including gardening and handy-man work. From time-to-time his services would be enlisted at the church as well, but tonight his task was to guard the prisoner. This turned out to be a lucky break for Rachel because although he was fairly adept at other tasks, the job of jailer was not well suited to him, and only a few minutes after the pastor had left, Joseph kicked back in the chair and fell fast asleep.

Rachel felt more at ease as Joseph's deep breathing remained at a steady pace. She would have rather been alone, but if someone had to stand guard, Joseph was a great choice. The door gently set into its latch and she made her way to the back. Once there she found the occupied cell and crouched down.

"David." She whispered, afraid of any excess noise. She hoped he would get the point of her intentional quietness and not shout out his response.

"Mother?" Her wish was fulfilled although she could barely hear him. "Is that you?"

"Yes it's me sweetheart. Are you okay? Have they hurt you?"

David was thrilled to hear his mother's voice. Until this moment he had not known her condition, but she was obviously okay if she was able to find him. He wanted to tell her everything that had occurred since they last saw each other, but as the words were about to pour from his mouth, he decided against it. He knew the love she felt for him would cause her to interfere if he revealed the truth. David wanted to protect her more than anything, and he felt the only way to accomplish that would be to lie.

"I'm okay. They have treated me well considering. The pastor is just looking for a way not to get in trouble. I think if we play along everything will be fine."

"What do you mean play along? What does he want us to do?"

"He will not let us tell our story to anyone. I was able to tell Mr. Cyrus, but he has been fooled and I doubt he believes me anymore. The pastor has to come up with a reason his nose is bruised and bloodied, and why my hand is hurt. So I have to plead guilty to hitting him. He will figure out the number of days I have to remain in here, and then everyone will go their own way. I know it's not the right thing, but it's what we will have to do.

Rachel's mind tried to process all that David was saying, but it was difficult. She knew the right thing to do. The pastor should be tried for his indiscretions, and he is the one who should be punished. She and David had done nothing wrong, but she also realized what they were up against. The pastor was no ordinary man. He was a fiendish manipulator who had spun his web of deception over the community for years. The foundation had been laid to weather any storm that might come his way. His word was unquestionable, and they had nothing but words as evidence on their side. The scenario David lay out before her might be the only sustainable option. David was a strong young man. His incarceration would not be difficult to bear. Their lives would be awkward since they would still be expected to attend church services and function as they normally would, and she would have to make sure to never be alone with the pastor again, but that was doable.

"Okay David. I don't like this, but it looks like there is no choice for us. I must leave now. It is too dangerous for me to be seen here, but I will speak with Constable Matthews tomorrow and figure out how this all will happen." The lies were not one-sided that evening since Rachel did not tell David she too was under arrest. "I will try to visit you again soon."

Mother and son said their goodbyes. David did not want to let her go, but he knew the danger of her being found visiting him. There was a tremendous bond between the two, and the selfless nature of their relationship was evident by the act of both trying to protect the other from further harm. Rachel left out the same door she entered, with the sleeping Joseph still unaware of her presence.

Demon Fire

Once settled back in the attic, Rachel actually fell asleep soon after her body became horizontal. She felt at ease knowing David was okay and that a plan of action was in place. While the situation was not the best possible, her mind was calm as she thought tomorrow held the chance of at least being better than today.

The next day Rachel awoke with a light tap on her door and Mrs. Mathew's voice announcing breakfast. After a few seconds of fumbling with the outside lock, a tray was brought in and set on a small table. Rachel thanked her keeper's wife and sat down to partake in the deliciousness before her. The breakfast was immaculate with fluffy eggs, perfectly cooked meat, bread, fruit, juice and coffee. Mrs. Mathew's was unfamiliar with the goings on of the day before. She was not privy to any of the discussions, and her husband did not confide in her any information. What she did know was that a guest resided in her house. An incarcerated guest but a guest none the less, and she would be treated as such. Rachel showed genuine gratitude for the food, and it was refreshing that someone was treating her with respect. The pastor had shown absolutely no respect yesterday when he tried to force himself on her, and the constable had shown very little when he locked her up. Now, with the new day, Rachel's outlook seemed a little brighter.

She was certain that she and David would emerge from this episode in their lives stronger and more determined than ever. They had overcome the most difficult of odds when they lost a husband and father, and together they would overcome this too.

Later that afternoon another knock on the attic door was heard. This knock was not from Mrs. Matthews though. There had been no lunch delivery, but with the grand feast from earlier it was not needed. Joseph's voice came from the other side of the door confirming she was dressed. As the door opened, she noticed Joseph had an entourage. Two rather large men stood directly behind him. Rachel did not know who these individuals were, but she assumed they had to be from one of the adjacent towns. The Constable, or more likely the pastor, must have sent for them the day before. It was well known that Pastor Sinclair had extensive dealings with surrounding communities. From time to time strangers were seen around the church grounds making deliveries or having meetings at the Constable's Office. No one knew the details of what went on with that business, but no one seemed to care either.

"You must come with us." Joseph was not rude with his language, but he was certainly abrupt and to the point.

"May I ask where we are going?"

"We are taking you home. Your warrant has been set aside and the charges have been dropped."

Demon Fire

Joy over-filled Rachel's heart. She was hesitant to believe David the night before when he gave an optimistic view of their situation, but now it seemed plausible. With all the charges against her dropped she assumed that he would serve a light sentence, and they soon would be free of this nightmare. Amazingly on the trip back to her house, she found herself humming an old song from childhood although, as she hummed away, it never occurred to her that they were taking the long way back. There was not much contrast in the scenery along this route since one tree looked the same as another, but one main difference was the fact that the path did not take them past the church.

The sanctuary room was fairly large. The church was the only building in town that had any style to its architecture, and this room in particular had unusually ornate wood and glasswork. The room was set with three rows of sturdy pews. Cushions were not readily available so a bare wooden plank served as the seat. The raised platform where the pulpit normally stood now held a round wooden table with three chairs set in a semicircle.

As David was led in from the back of the room he saw Pastor Sinclair, Constable Matthews and to his surprise Cyrus Williams sitting around the table. Escorting David were two outsiders he had never seen before. One walked in front and one walked at his side holding onto the left arm. The hit to his head from the day before still had him wobbly, and that was compounded by a total lack of sleep from the night before. David realized the gravity of his situation about the time Rachel had departed, and the remainder of his night was filled with hatred, anxiety and plenty of tears, but no rest. The anxiety had been manifested by fear of the unknown. The hate was focused on the pastor and by proxy, the church as well. The church now seemed a foreign place to him. The assault on his mother from the day before happened here and David was feeling increasingly like the evil that oozed from the pastor somehow coincided with the church itself.

When David and his escorts made it to the front of the sanctuary, the Constable motioned for them to take a seat on the middle pew closest to the front. Once seated, Pastor Sinclair spoke.

"The proceedings of this court will begin, and the case against David Devlin will be heard. It is acknowledged that the accused Mr. Devlin is present with us along with Constable Mathews and our community member witness Cyrus Williams. Constable, will you please read the updated charges?"

Constable Mathews rose and read from the warrant that was hastily written that morning after the pastor's late night meeting with David.

Demon Fire

"In the name of the Office of Constable written in the Town of Haniford on this twenty-third day of May, it has been sworn by a distinguished and outstanding member of our community, whose image and word is impeccable in both poise and dignity, that the following has truthfully occurred the day before this. David Devlin and his mother Rachel Devlin were seen by the eye of a witness to have been in the act of unholy relations with one another. The act of carnal knowledge which occurred between the two having been forced by the son David Devlin in an act directly at odds against God and his teachings concludes in the charge of heresy."

David's head sank into his hands. He knew the arrangement, and he had made his decision, but the words spoken aloud were almost too much to take. He took a deep breath and raised his head again with his heart hardened and his dignity intact swearing he would show no shame in the face of false charges. The eyes of Cyrus could be seen staring straight at him with a hurtful look on his face. The charges had not been completely read the day before in the Constable's office, but they had been changed since then anyway so to Cyrus the idea that David sat here accused of forcing himself on Rachel in that way was more than could be imagined.

Pastor Sinclair rose from his seat in the middle of the table with the Constable to his left and Cyrus to his right.

"David Devlin rise." David rose from his seat with the help of his handlers. "The charges have been read in open court with witness present. You may plead Guilty to the charges and proceed to sentencing, or you may plead Not Guilty; whereas we will commence with a trial. How will you plead?

Silence filled the room. No one stirred and no one spoke. All eyes fixed on David and the tension was palpable. Everyone knew the stakes and the seriousness of the charges. The town had never dealt with such a situation as this before, and it would surely be changed because of it. David, however, was not interested in long-term effects for the town. He focused on the task at hand. Saving his mother was paramount, and the only way he could foresee that happening was to speak the word that carried no truth.

"Guilty." The word was spoken without emotion and without fear. An audible gasp came from Cyrus, and Constable Mathews felt a shiver run through his body. Even the pastor seemed visibly shaken by the word although it was expected. David stood straight and proud. When the pastor spoke again it was after a long pause to regroup.

"David do you understand the seriousness of the charges and more importantly the severity of the punishment?"

"Yes I do." David said as his gaze focused on the pastor.

Demon Fire

"And you plead Guilty to the charge of heresy, and you admit to doing what has been said you have done?"

"Yes."

"This court will accept the plea of Guilty from David Devlin to the charges presented." Pastor Sinclair was thrilled with the result, but he knew showing emotion would not be in his best interest and therefore he remained professional. He also knew that he would need the support from ones other than himself. "Constable Matthews, as the chief law enforcement officer of the community, do you accept the plea of Guilty?"

"I do." The Constable's eyes locked onto the paper in front of him. He would not look at the other members sitting at the table nor would he look at the accused.

"Cyrus, being the designated witness, do you accept the plea of Guilty?"

Cyrus' eyes never left David. The somber look was still upon his face as he answered. "This entire episode is beyond my comprehension. My mind cannot make any sense of the transgressions that are said to have happened, but I also cannot dispute the words that have just now exited this young man's mouth. I will not doubt a verdict that has no opposition, so it is with a heavy heart that I must say yes. I accept the plea of Guilty."

"Very well." The pastor could barely contain his joy. There had been indiscretions in his past, but the fear of retribution had always kept things under wraps. This time was different. This time there was a witness. Without a believable confession there would have always been doubt, and doubt was not something that would sustain the pastor's influence within the community. "The law of heresy has but one sentence available. David Devlin you are hereby sentenced to death by fire, and the sentence to be carried out without hesitation."

Cyrus stood up from the table. "Pastor my job here is complete. You needed a witness to this proceeding, and I reluctantly obliged since I had become a part of this issue yesterday and felt that I needed to see it through. I will not be a part of anything further, and I beg your leave."

"That is fine Cyrus. I appreciate your help in the matter. You will not be obligated to witness the end result, and I thank you for your cooperation." Looking back to David, the pastor proceeded with instructions for the others present. David was taken outside the church and escorted past the gallows deep into the woods along a makeshift trail. Pastor Sinclair led the procession with Constable Matthews in the rear. David's two escorts remained at his side to help along the way.

The trail opened into a clearing where a post had been set into the ground. Along the bottom edge of the post laid sticks and logs of various sizes set in an inverted cone shape. David's escorts led him straight to the post without fanfare. Amazingly he showed no fear. His aching head was held high as he was determined not to give the pastor the pleasure of seeing him scared. As he was placed with his back to the post and strapped down, the pungent odor of an oil-based liquid hung in the air. The wood had been treated with some sort of flammable liquid which seemed advantageous to David. He assumed that the fire would consume him quickly and he could leave the cruelty he faced here, for the afterlife the pastor had spoken so fervently of during his sermons.

No one spoke a word as the two outsiders backed away with one walking in the direction of a small fire that had been smoldering off to the side. Once there, he reached down and picked up a torch and held it to the embers. As the torch lit the man looked at the pastor for a signal. The pastor stood with the Constable approximately thirty feet away from where David was bound. A nod to the torch bearer and the torment began.

David could feel the heat on his feet and calves through his clothing as soon as the flames began to rise. He steadied his resolve, closed his eyes, and turned his mind to his mother. Her beauty and caring had sustained him for as long as he could remember. She had borne a great loss in his father's passing, but there was no stopping her determination to see him survive and thrive in this cruel and unforgiving world. The pain was now growing, but David bit his lip and tensed his muscles. No one would hear him scream. He would stay silent and reverent for his mother. His love for Rachel knew no boundaries, and he was happy to make this sacrifice for her freedom.

David's eyes opened with a snap. The shrill scream tore unwillingly at his throat and could be heard for miles around as the fire lifted past his thighs and began tearing at his abdomen. The heat became unbearable as the clothing and flesh melted into each other while the thoughts of his mother's beauty and love vanished. He no longer cared for her or any other reality of the Earth. All he knew was pain. Excruciating pain that did not relinquish its grip as his flesh gave way to the heat. The outside of his body was reshaping itself into a new form as the inside tried to compensate by increasing his heart rate and respirations - but to no avail. The blood the heart pumped was leaving the body through the opening skin and the air the lungs inspired was used solely to vibrate the vocal cords into the piercing sounds of anguish that resonated from his mouth.

At this point the witnesses to the event had become deeply disturbed. No one present, including the pastor, had ever seen a spectacle such as this. The unrelenting torture became uncomfortable to watch and everyone secretly wished for an end to the proceedings. A quick conclusion to the misery would not come, however, since the wood and oil of a small fire such as this did not provide enough smoke and gas release to suffocate a victim, and therefore the flames would be required to finish the job. The cause of death in David's case would more than likely be from the loss of bodily fluids or total internal organ failure. These causes, while still fatal, would take time, and there was much suffering left to endure.

David's eyes remained open as he looked at the pastor. As the pain radiated through his upper torso and neck his hate and loathing for the man increased. This hatred grew for the person and everything he stood for including the church he had led. David gazed at the one who had done this to him as his eyes began to lose their consistency to the heat. The pastor along with everyone else, had looked away by this point, and pride was the only thing preventing them from covering their ears as well. No one could believe his throat still had enough consistency to continue making noise. But the screams persisted and the memories of those sounds would be what haunted the witnesses most often in the years to come.

In the end David's pain finally subsided. The burns had singed most of the nerve endings and the sensations that remained were not processed by the brain any longer. He could still see the pastor standing in front of him with his head lowered. The eyes did not transmit his sight, but instead the pastor's image had been imprinted in his memory as plain as a picture painted there. The agony that he had endured had warped David's entire sense of being. He was no longer a young man of eighteen who worked hard and cared for other people, and he was no longer a creature of this earth. Hate and pain had transformed him into something different; something terrible; something that took hold as he left the conscious world and died.

David awoke to a state of nothingness. His senses were alive, but their use was foreign to him. He could see - yet he had no eyes. He could feel - yet he had no skin. There was no pain or suffering, but there was also no love or affection. He was living through his mind's eye, but could not manipulate the world around him. He did recognize his location. It was the last place he had been in his previous form. The area had been cleared of all remnants of his final day and there was no one to be found. To his dismay the townsfolk seemed to intentionally avoid the place, and it would be long after they had passed and the river which was located miles away was dammed that anyone would venture his way again. Until then he had time to get familiar with the nothingness that surrounded him. He also had time to contemplate his revenge for the hurt, pain and madness that his new situation would bring.

Chapter 12
Flames of Freedom

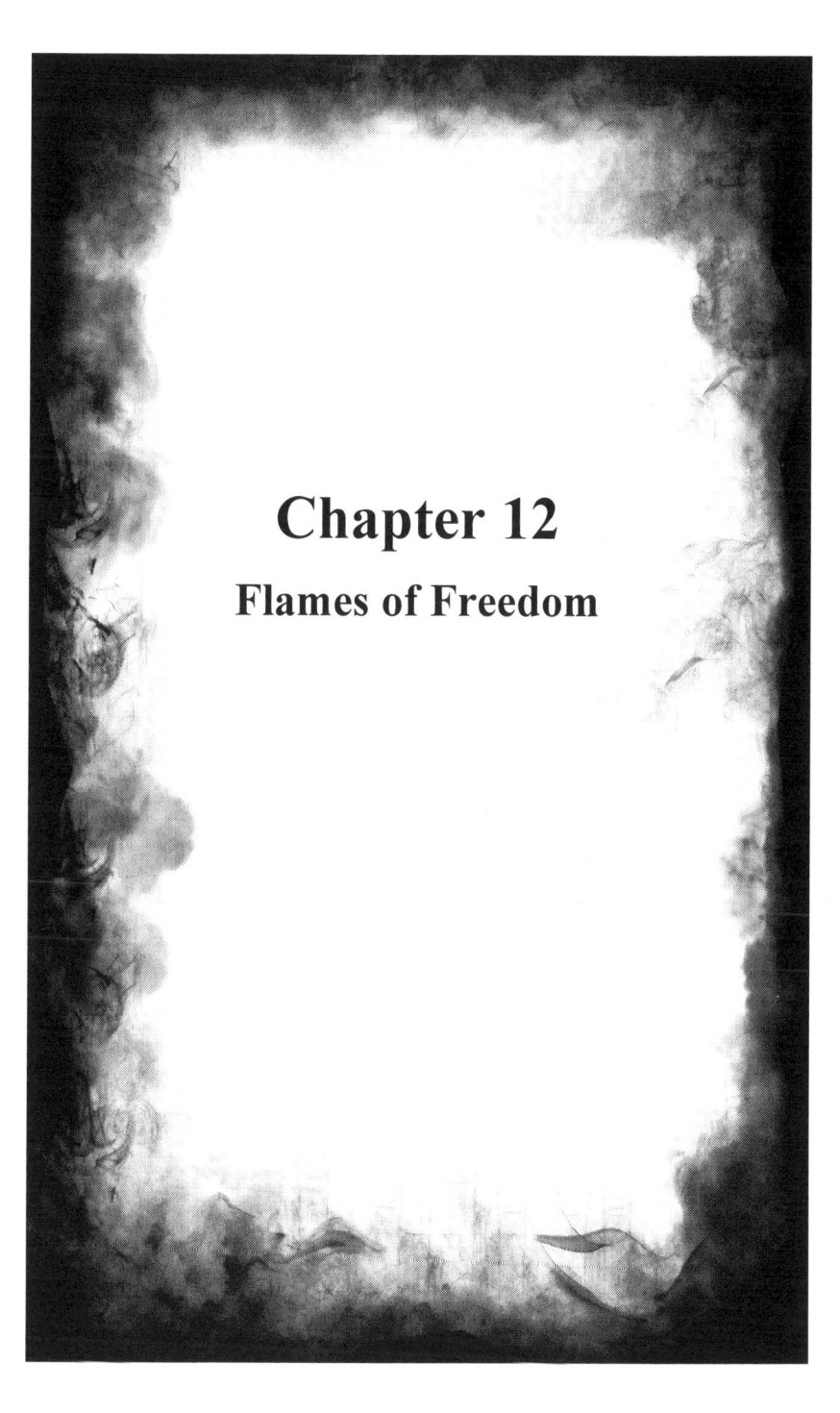

Chris Cumbie

Demon Fire

The Tri County Historical Society was located just down the road from Jake's office. The two story brick structure was a place he had been to occasionally for special events but little else. Janice Forton was an elderly woman with perfectly curled hair. She wore the obligatory glasses, which rode on the edge of her nose and were thought by most people to be used only as a prop. She had been the curator of the place the last twenty-five years, and she had enjoyed every minute of time spent there. Most people in the community were unaware that a repository of the past was within their boundaries, and the ones that knew about it were uninterested and rarely visited. The local government did not show concern for the establishment either save for the once-a-year budget item that was approved with little debate or concern.

As far as Ms. Janice, as she liked to be called, was concerned, the history of the area was the most important thing in her life and should be the most important in everyone else's too. She knew getting people excited about history was not an easy task, however, especially when that history was not always interesting. She tried to drum up community interest with activities and special events, but visitors remained sparse. Because of this disinterest Ms. Janice was ecstatic when Jake entered the building and asked about researching the archives. She could not be sure that she remembered when the last person had come in and actually wanted to stay and go through the records, but someone was there now, and the moment would not be wasted.

Jake found himself set up in a medium-sized conference room where note pads, pencils, pens and a laptop computer were brought in for his use. Ms. Janice would be at his beck and call for any information needed and within the first hour, books and files littered the table around him. The data Charlie mined from his computer bank was extensive, but most of the local history would not have been uploaded into any data system so delving into the hard copied world of the Historical Society was in order.

Jake's work proceeded along well with Ms. Janice breaking into a sprint every time he mentioned needing a book or paperwork from storage; and she constantly brought him something to drink or snack on.

At the top of the third hour of progress, a breakthrough occurred. As Jake focused on a text of local religious history he suddenly stopped and scribbled notes. He assumed that an audible noise of excitement must have emanated from him at some point because Ms. Janice rushed around the corner and into the room.

"What's the matter?" Janice asked.

"Oh nothing. Everything is fine. I think I have found what I was looking for."

Ms. Janice was both joyous and dejected. She was more than pleased in her ability to provide the Society's resources to someone that actually needed them, but she was sad that her little adventure was ending. Jake was putting his things away and thanking her for the help. She was unsure when, if ever, the next visitor might pass through with a need, but one thing was certain. As usual, she would be available and ready to help when that day occurred.

A few minutes later Jake entered his vehicle and proceeded down the road. He had been skeptical that he would be able to corroborate any of the information gained from Charlie, but there it was in plain English sitting in a book at the Tri County Historical Society. Still unsure of what he was thinking or doing, Jake's SUV pulled onto the scene of the first fire at the Life of God Church. Since the incident, the building had been left untouched other than a beam or two falling or a bit of foundation crumbling.

Jake assumed the insurance adjustors had been there already. He hoped the paperwork would not take too long so the demolition or repair could begin. Seeing people move on with their lives after a fire always gave him a sense of hope for the future.

After a moment of staring at the charred remains of the former house of worship, Jake's search began. The information obtained from Charlie and the Historical Society was fairly specific about location so he started by fanning out from the church in a circular pattern. He had confidence that what he was looking for would be easily found. After a couple of hours, however, his certainty started to waiver. There was no sign of what he sought as each square inch of area was checked. After the sun set, he used a flashlight, which was good for focusing attention on areas that might be glanced over in full daylight. Still, nothing was noticed. Jake sat on a tree stump at the wood line. He was disheartened, and after a few minutes he pulled out his phone and dialed the only contact that could help him in this situation.

"Hey. What's up?" Sarah's voice was good to hear on the other end of the line.

"Well, I'm just finishing up with the most non-productive day in the history of the world." Jake's voice was unusually perky which did not match his dull feeling. He assumed just talking to Sarah was making him feel better already.

"Do you want to tell me about it?"

"Yeah, but not over the phone. Do you think we could meet somewhere?" Jake figured she might not be up to a late evening get together, but he took a shot anyway. He wanted to vent about his frustrations with the investigations, but doing so on the phone while sitting on a stump with a burned out church as a backdrop was not what he had in mind.

"Of course we can. I haven't eaten yet so somewhere with food would be nice."

"Great. How about Angelino's?"

"Wow! Angelino's? What's the occasion?" Sarah asked.

"Nothing special. I've just had a rough day, and I want some good food and good company."

"Well I'm not going to turn that offer down. I need to get ready though. Angelino's calls for a dress and heels."

"Yeah, I'm about to head home and change too. It's late so do you want to just meet there?" Jake would have rather gone to Sarah's house and picked her up. It would be the proper thing to do since he asked her to go, and in some crazy way it would seem more like a date. It was getting late though so meeting up at the restaurant would be the better choice.

"Okay Jake. I'll see you there in about an hour?"

"An hour it is." Jake was excited to see Sarah, and to see her in a dress and heels would be amazing. Angelino's was an unusual place. The establishment was housed in three attached buildings with a fine dining restaurant, lounge area and a large dance floor. The cover charge, food and drinks were pricy, but the quality meals and fun atmosphere kept it busy most evenings. Sarah was excited to go, and she threw herself into the shower as soon as the phone call ended then practically danced around the closet looking for the perfect outfit. As she placed a slinky black party dress against her and stood in front of the full-length mirror, a thought came that extra care should be taken tonight. Her excitement was not only about going out and having a good time, something she rarely did, but it was bolstered because she would be with Jake. The agreement she made with herself, not to let feelings get in the way of helping him with this case was slowly crumbling, and as the dress made its way down over her perfectly curved body, she swore that it would stay on until she was back home and alone.

Jake arrived first and grabbed a table close to the entrance so he could see when Sarah arrived. He was a little anxious. Although the events of the past few days ran through his head, the idea that this might turn out to be an actual date was present as well. The nervous energy only increased when his evening companion walked through the front door, and he pushed his chair back with such force that it teetered precariously on its back legs before resting again on the floor. Jake had never remembered seeing such beauty before. Sarah's hair was full and glowing. The makeup was perfect and the dress. He could not get over the dress. It fit perfectly, revealing just enough leg and cleavage to garner attention, but covering enough to be classy.

Sarah was equally impressed with Jake. He wore a dark form-fitting suit with a vest that added just the right touch of style. Her heart fluttered as she turned the corner and saw him awkwardly rising to greet her. Keeping the promise she made to herself would not be an easy task tonight, but she was ready for good food and dancing so she set the thoughts of her future behavior to the side. As they embraced Jake leaned in and whispered in her ear.

"You look amazing."

"Thanks. You look pretty amazing yourself." Jake came around and pulled out the adjacent seat. They both focused on the menu for a few minutes before ordering, and small talk filled the time until the food arrived. As they ate Jake broached the subject of the investigations.

"Well it was an interesting day to say the least." Jake began. "I went to see Charlie for lunch, and you should see the place. It was unreal. You have been in the comic book store before haven't you?"

"Yes. I've stopped by to see Charlie before. It seems like a cool spot."

"Next time you go, tell him to show you upstairs. It's surprising." Jake described the apartment loft and the personal library and computer set up as well as the career path that Charlie had chosen.

"That is impressive. Who would have guessed that our local comic shop was a cover for a worldwide covert intelligence operation? So I guess Detective Maxwell was right after all. Speaking with Charlie was a good idea. Did he give you any leads?"

"I guess you could say that. I don't know. I'm still not sure what to think of it all. I'm a realist, and there was nothing real about what he showed me."

"What do you mean?" Sarah was excited to hear about his interaction with Charlie, but this conversation seemed strange.

"Okay. I'm not sure how else to say it. He said we are dealing with a demon. More specifically, a fire demon." Jake paused for a reaction but none came. Sarah sat expressionless so he continued. "I know, it sounds crazy to me too, but he pulled up so much information. There were reports from all over the world with similar situations. Charlie said there was some sort of demon that traveled through fire and passed from person to person setting the churches ablaze." Again there was a pause, but this time there was a response from Sarah.

"Wow. That's insane Jake. I'm sorry Charlie did nothing to help. I was hopeful that something good would come of your meeting although I can't say what that might have been. At least you were able to get a good laugh out of it while you were there. I hope you didn't hurt his feelings too much."

Jake's head slumped. "That's not exactly how things went down. It sounds stupid now, but he really had me convinced that his premise could be a possibility."

"No way! The most by-the-book, practical guy I know - believing in the supernatural?"

"Yeah, I realize how it looks. I guess I was at my wits end and ready to believe anything."

"It's okay. I'm just giving you a hard time. Even if it sounds crazy, keeping an open mind can be advantageous, and you said he had information about other situations similar to ours?"

"Yes. He pulled up many similar instances. I think I got caught up in the idea." He was impressed at Sarah's understanding of the situation. It would have been natural to look down on him for letting such notions enter his mind, but other than the initial playful joking, her demeanor showed a good deal of care and compassion. At that moment Jake wanted to kiss her so badly that he could hardly contain himself, but her feelings had been made clear the other day, and he was not about to step out of bounds.

"So continue with your story."

"Okay. We were looking through all of this information coming across the monitor screens. Charlie seemed to be taking it all in so I stood back and watched him work. After a few moments he turned to me and said that I was dealing with a demon that associated itself with fire somehow. He thought I needed to find the beginning to get to the end. Something like a Point of Origin I guess you might say. Charlie had his mind set that the churches were the connection, so whatever this thing was or is, must have begun there. He told me that most of the demons he had heard about in the past had manifested from real people who had such great emotional stress during death that the soul could not disperse. Charlie surmised that a tragedy must have occurred either at the Life of God Church itself or on the land that it sits on at some point in history. He pulled up as much information as he had, but could not pinpoint specific instances in the area so it was suggested that I visit the Historical Society and search through the records there. I feel so foolish. I was excited and really believed that I was on the right track. Looking back now I was just dumb."

"Don't beat yourself up." Sarah said reassuringly. "We were told to think outside of the box. Even a wild goose chase could lead to something positive. Tell me what happened at the Historical Society. I bet Ms. Janice was thrilled to see you there."

"Now if anything positive came from my adventures today, it is the fact that I was able to make Ms. Janice's day." Jake managed a smile as he continued. "So I took Charlie's advice, and to my surprise there was a ton of well-organized history about the area in that place. I had books and papers spread out trying to find anything that might deal with something tragic or that dealt with fire. Charlie felt that fire was the key, and it must have been involved in whatever happened in the past. As I dove into the research, several historical fires popped up but nothing of significance stood out. Then I stumbled across a story in a file about an old forgotten town called Haniford. The town existed back during the colonial period, but although it prospered for generations, the community did not last into modern times. Not much had been written about the place, but there was one paragraph that spoke of a young man who had gone against the church and was burned alive for his crimes."

"Oh wow Jake. That sounds like exactly what you were looking for. I mean it's still a bunch of bull, but Charlie was right about a tragedy with fire occurring in the area. You have to give him credit for that much at least. Did the paperwork say where the town was located?"

"Not specifically. I saw the year 1855 written on one of the papers so I assume the story had been passed down for many years before someone jotted it down. It seemed from the writing that the town had already dried up by then. It talked about the large stone foundation of the original church building though so I found a book on historical churches from the 1950's and sure enough, the Haniford church was mentioned and the building's stone foundation had been intact at that time."

"That is amazing." The story interested Sarah although she assumed by the way it was being presented that the ending would not be fulfilling. It sounded a little like a treasure hunt had been in progress, and she understood why Jake had gotten caught up in something so preposterous.

"It seemed amazing at the time. I tore out of there and headed straight to the first church fire. I just knew the ancient foundation would be there. I assumed Charlie's theory would be proven, and I would at least have a place to start figuring out these fires."

"I'm assuming that is where the story takes a turn for the worse." Sarah said.

"Yep. I searched all over that place. The stone foundation was obviously not part of the existing church, but the building itself became my starting point. I fanned out from there, but I found nothing. Not even two rocks stacked on top of each other. Absolutely nothing. That's when it hit me how much of the day had been wasted on chasing a fantasy."

Demon Fire

"Okay it was a wasted day, we can both agree on that, but there is no use dwelling on it. Let's focus on the here and now. You are here with me and we have some excellent food, great company and a dance floor that has our name on it."

Jake was pleased that she was so understanding, and the idea of moving with her to the rhythm of the music immediately put him in a better mood. They finished the meal then headed through the bar to the far side of the establishment where several couples were already on the dance floor. Jake and Sarah were quite talented when it came to dancing. Both had taken lessons in the past and most of the steps were familiar to them. They both were glad that the food had not bogged them down too much since they did not step off of the floor until almost an hour had passed. They walked over to the bar area holding hands which seemed nice to Jake although there had been plenty of physical contact during the dancing. Each had driven there, so they decided to order soft drinks instead of alcohol. Neither were opposed to drinking, but losing their jobs due to a night of fun was not something either one wanted to chance.

"My goodness. I haven't danced like that in forever." Sarah said as she slumped into her seat.

"I know. I'll probably feel it in the morning. I'm sure you will be up early running with no soreness at all." Jake added.

"Yeah. You might be right. Whew, that was a workout though. We need to do this more often."

"You mean go out on a date?" Jake was in the moment and did not think things through before he spoke. He was certain that his question would kill the mood, but it had already left his lips.

"Yes. I mean go out on a date. Tonight has been great. I've really enjoyed being around you the past couple of days. Even though the circumstances haven't been pleasant, it has been nice to have a partner."

The statement from Sarah was unexpected, but welcome. "I've enjoyed being with you as well. I honestly don't believe that I could have gotten through all of this by myself. Just having someone to lean on and be there for me has been amazing, and of course you are pretty amazing anyway."

"You're trying to make me blush now." Sarah said.

"No I mean it. You are a smart, funny, strong, beautiful, independent woman. You have everything going for you."

"Well I have one thing going for me."

"What's that?"

"I have my second wind." With a grin, she took Jake by the hand and another thirty minutes of dancing followed. There were a couple of slow songs intermixed among the playlist and the two held each other tight as they swayed to the music. At the end of the last song Jake slipped his left hand around her waist and paused just a second before gently pulling her toward him for a kiss. He was unsure of the outcome, but it was worth a try. Moving forward her eyes glistened and her head tilted slightly, and as their lips drew nearer, Jake knew he had chosen wisely. When they met, his right hand gently pushed its way around under her neck. Jake pulled Sarah in closer to the point that no room was left in between their bodies as the kiss continued. The forceful, yet gentle, embrace was both unexpected and exhilarating for Sarah, and as their lips parted, and Jake opened his eyes, he could see a smile gleaming from her face to go along with the flushed look. Leaning in, she whispered in his ear.

"Would you like to come over to my place tonight?"

Jake was stunned. He did not know what might have changed to break through her wall. As it turned out she was not entirely sure herself, but neither one seemed to care at the moment.

"Yes." Jake said. "I can stop by."

"Good. Maybe we will start a new point of origin for ourselves. Just give me a twenty minute head start."

Sarah departed with a long hug and a kiss on the cheek. Jake waited at the bar while sipping on his soda trying not to focus too much on the clock on the wall, but the wait was excruciating. His feelings had gone into overdrive the past few days. The night had been great so far, and the fact that it did not have to end was more than he could have hoped for.

As the time crept by a sense of nervous anticipation overtook Jake, and he quickly paid the tab and began the trip to Sarah's. The full twenty minutes had not passed, but his plan was to drive slowly. That plan failed, however, as the vehicle traveled down the road pushing eighty. The windows were cracked and a cool breeze blew against his face as a random seventies rock song played on the radio. As the music thumped and the mind wandered, a thought made Jake pause for a moment; and then suddenly his right foot slammed against the brake pedal and pushed it almost to the floor as the car fishtailed to a stop.

Sarah had mentioned starting a new point of origin in their relationship. The phrase was intended to be playful as it related to both their relationship and their line of work, but now it had Jake questioning how much the tragic and unusual circumstances recently had clouded his judgment.

Charlie told him that all of his data led back to the first church fire, but that was not the point of origin. The first sign of strange occurrences began at the cabin on Talbot Lake. The initial fire where Cole was lost had all the anomalies seen in the subsequent church fires, but somehow Jake had not added that fact into his thought process. It all made sense to him now although he was still unsure about the paranormal aspects of everything, but he figured there was one way to find out for certain. A quick text asking for a rain check was sent to Sarah. Canceling the continuation of their date was not something he took pleasure in, but he had to find out for his own peace of mind whether his theory would play out or not.

The car spun around and another twenty minutes later the burned-out cabin on Talbot Lake was in sight. The procedure would be the same as the last search. The foundation of the former church was not part of the cabin structure so with flashlight in hand Jake moved in a distinct pattern close to the water's edge before turning and heading toward the woods on the far side of the building. Several yards into the trees he stopped the sweeping motion of the light and stood with his mouth open in amazement. There in the distance he saw the unmistakable outline of a rock wall approximately two feet high. The rocks had crumbled in places and the passing centuries had taken a toll on the foundation, but there was no doubt that what Jake found were the remnants of a building from years past. Right in front of him - right where it should be. His practical mind was gone, and there was no inclination of bringing the world that Jake had known his entire life back.

All of the strange occurrences were now explained. The way the cabin fire forced itself from the bathroom through to the bedroom using a small hole. The burn Chief Taylor suffered when the fire pushed down upon him. The inexplicable arson that occurred with the Chief as the only suspect. The fire from each of the churches acting erratically. Firefighter Wade setting the second church fire with no evident motive and not remembering any part of it. It all made sense now, while at the same time, not making any sense at all. There had to be some sort of parasite living in or through the fire that passed among normal people to continue its carnage. As crazy as it all sounded, that hypothesis had been tested and was now proven in Jake's mind. The tragedy happened many years ago at the very spot of this modern day cabin. The demon, or whatever it was, had passed into Chief Taylor when the flames brushed his shoulder; and then into Firefighter Wade the same way. Jake paused in his thoughts as he played events back in his head, and a second realization presented itself. There was another. Pastor Stephens of the First Christian Church of Newton. He had thought nothing about it. A burn to the finger that did not require medical attention was not a real concern. Sarah had not even noted it in her report. He probably wouldn't have either. It was such a small injury that a bandage had been used more for precaution than need. But it was a burn. The demon had found a third body, and there was nothing stopping him from burning again.

Demon Fire

Jake was in his personal car, but being a good investigator meant he still had the required tools of the trade inside the trunk, and a drafting compass and map were quickly retrieved. He realized now, the vehicle of destruction was Pastor Stephens, but the location of the next target was not known. He placed the point of the compass on the spot where the cabin was located. The attached pencil was then set at the first church fire and a circle was drawn. This task continued for the next church. It was easy to see that the two churches were the closest ones to the cabin. Jake scanned out from the last drawn circle and there it was - Bolson Ferry Church. A third circle was completed, and Jake could see that Bolson Ferry was next in line. The church sat inside Deer Creek County to the south of where he was. It was one of the oldest churches in the area, but there was no permanent congregation there. The building sat off of the main road, and other than the occasional singing or revival, it was seldom used.

Jake attached his duty pistol and badge on his belt and headed off towards the presumed next target. As he pulled onto the road heading to the church, a quick glance at his phone showed that Sarah had not responded to his last text. He was not sure if she would forgive him for standing her up, but he felt compelled to play this scenario out. He wanted to get to the church and then figure out a way to set up surveillance. The problem with that would be coming up with a good reason for the Sheriff's Office. He was more than confident that an application to surveil a fire demon that traveled the area starting arson fires would not go over well.

As he wound his way down the long dirt road, the church crept into view. The small building had no steeple, and the only outward appearance of it being a house of worship was the sign next to the road designating it as such. The exterior wallboards were freshly painted white, and the landscaping had been well maintained. Bushes and flowers were planted around the area to coincide with its manicured lawn. As Jake's view passed over the area, his heart jumped. He had expected to find the church empty, but next to a large tree to the side of the building sat a vehicle. Jake turned off his lights as he slowed to a crawl and pulled to the side of the road a safe distance away. Normal procedure would be to call in backup and wait, but this was anything but a normal situation so Jake exited his car and did the only thing he knew to do. He drew his pistol and moved cautiously toward the church. A sliver of moon lit the way although its shine was not enough to expose his location. Beads of sweat appeared on his brow as he got to the outside wall and crouched down to wait and listen. No sound could be heard and the window-blinds were pulled so nothing could be seen from his vantage point.

Demon Fire

Moving to the back of the property he noticed a door that, as expected, had been forced open. The door was shut now so Jake moved the back of his hand over it to feel for any heat. No smoke or flames were visible, but he did not want to take any chances. The door was cool so he slowly pulled it open and entered the church finding himself standing in a small vestibule with an entrance to his left and one to the right. A strong smell permeated through the air and Jake knew a fire had already been set. The door to his left was warm and crackling noises could be heard from the other side. At this point it was too late to stop the church from burning. Preventing the next church fire was now his only option, so he moved to the door on the right. Again he checked for heat and finding none opened the door to the sanctuary. As he entered, the pistol in his hands raised and the sights lined up with Pastor Stephens' chest.

"Hello Jake." The voice was guttural and harsh, but the words were easily understood. Jake had only met the pastor twice before and was unsure that he would have remembered his name, but he knew it was not the preacher speaking. "I see the look of confusion on your face. It is logical. You are here with me now so there are certain things you must have figured out. Your investigative training has paid off well." The words and voice were much more understandable than when David first entered Chief Taylor's mind. The manipulation of the body's senses and functions occurred now with little to no effort on his part.

"You need to lay face down on the floor and spread your arms to the side!" Jake's voice was loud and determined, but unwavering and clear even with the fear building up in him.

David raised the hands of the pastor who was an older balding gentleman with a slightly hunched over stature. The antithesis of scary except for the fact that a demon lived inside.

"Now get on the floor and spread out your arms!" Jake repeated as only the first command had been followed.

"I have changed bodies a few times as you know Jake, but I still have the memories of each, and nothing I have seen from Chief Taylor about your demeanor would indicate that I am in any danger. In other words, there's no way you are going to shoot the sweet old Pastor Stephens." An all knowing grin spread across the pastor's face as his hands lowered to his sides. Jake kept his gun pointed, but dropped it an inch as his eyes lifted off of the sites and settled over the barrel.

"That's what I thought. Now what are we going to do about this situation Jake? I mean you have a job to do, but unfortunately for you that is contrary to my needs."

"Your needs are not my concern. My only concern is that you follow my orders and lay on the floor."

Demon Fire

"Well you and I both know that is not going to happen, so the question is where do we go from here? You have a gun, but are unable to use it. I on the other hand have an aged body that is useless in battle. So we seem to be at an impasse. Of course we cannot forget about the fire I have started in the next room. I am not sure it will wait for our deliberation to end before it decides to join us."

"Look." Jake began as the gun in his hand shook slightly. "I understand you are angry about what happened to you in the past but..." The sentence trailed off as David brought the pastor's shoulders back and stood up as high as the elderly spine would allow.

"You understand nothing!" The voice was stronger and more pronounced than it should have been coming out of that body. "Your mind is weak. There has never been tragedy in your life such as I have seen." Jake was fearful of what might happen although he was not sure what a demon in an old man's body could do. "Do you not realize that I have died once already?" David channeled all of his anger into the old pastor's voice. "Can you imagine flesh slipping away from your body? Feeling every flame as it completed its destruction, and the only relief turns out to be a never ending state of loneliness and despair? How dare you think your feeble brain could fathom any part of what I have been through!"

"Let me tell you something Jake. Let me tell you what I thought about while the flames ate away at my skin. I thought of everything and everyone I would have given up to lessen the pain. I cannot bring myself to repeat the horrible things that traveled through my head. Those thoughts have haunted me since that day, but one thought was able to sustain me. The thought of my revenge against the one person who orchestrated my sorrow stayed forefront in my mind while I burned and then while I waited. Our exalted Pastor Sinclair caused my pain, and although I knew I could never exact revenge against him personally, I would be able to destroy what he stood for which as you have figured out is why we are standing here together in this place."

"I have been planning this for generations, and once I began occupying others, I opened myself up to an abundance of information that would help me on my journey. Of course I could not have planned any better to have the leader of the fire brigade as my first host, but I took complete advantage of it nonetheless; and, of course, the fact that I have been able to jump from person to person has kept anyone from catching on. Anyone that is, except for you my industrious Jake. I remember you at the hospital asking questions. Questions about the fire and how puzzled you were at the inconsistencies of its behavior. I didn't imagine at the time that you might figure everything out, but you have, and that means you must be stopped. Or better yet instead of stopped, maybe used."

Jake still had his pistol at the low-ready. He knew there was danger somehow, but he was still unaware of how this feeble unarmed man might bring him harm. The smoke billowed out from around the door that led to the fire, and Jake figured it would not be long until it broke free and entered their space. He was trying to determine how much time they had and what his next move would be as David's host finished speaking and suddenly made a break for the back of the sanctuary. The aged body was not built for speed, but it moved toward the fire door with a forced exuberance that was surprising. Jake hesitated before running after him. He was unsure of what might happen and this pause meant that David reached his destination with plenty of time to spare. As the door to the fire flung open Jake remembered the statement about him being used, and realized what was taking place. The only power available to David lay in the flames, and who better to be the next host than a fire investigator with all the knowledge needed to continue the quest unabated. Jake quickly holstered his weapon. He knew all of his strength and speed would be needed. To his left was the still opened door in which he entered, and Jake determined this would be his escape route. A quick glance behind him saw Pastor Stephen's body enter the fire, and as Jake's feet began to move a wall of flames rushed out. The heat could be felt behind him as he went, and he knew a small burn was all it would take for his own possession to occur.

The flames had a tight grouping that appeared as a cylindrical shape emanating from the open doorway. The movements were unnatural. The heat and smoke did not rise and spread but remained in the current trajectory until a right-angle turn was taken as it headed for Jake who stayed just ahead of the pace. As the fire moved, a sound could be heard that was not associated with any fire he had ever known. The noise was animalistic, and must have been what Chief Taylor had described hearing at the cabin. There was no time to think about such things though. Through the first door he went, slamming it behind thinking the barrier would slow the approaching fire. This theory was short lived, however, as the hinges gave way to the force, and the door crashed into the far wall. The flames took another sharp turn, which brought them precariously close as Jake made his move toward the exit. He did not pray often, but a quick "God give me strength" went up as he leaped further than he would have ever imagined. A perfect barrel roll onto the ground and he was up with his legs moving as fast as possible under him. Jake did not stop or look back until he was at his car again surveying the scene. From this vantage point he could see the flames had scorched the grass at least twenty feet past the house before running out of fuel. A quick check of his body produced a sigh of relief since no burns were found.

David was beyond furious, but his most extreme emotion was fear. He had failed in his attempt to enter a new host body, and he worried that his last host would not be viable after entering the flames. His last hope was lying on the floor in the adjacent room, and as the flames entered and crept close to the exposed left arm, a glimmer of hope arose that the body might yet be usable since the shell was still in relatively good shape. That hope faded, however, as the skin blistered and he entered Pastor Stephens once more. There was no sign of consciousness although the unconscious mind was still active. David tried with all of his might to make the systems function but to no avail. The pastor was better off since no pain would accompany him on the journey home, but for David it was tragic. His host was passing and there were no more options. He raced through the memories to find some nugget of information that might help, but it was clear that no piece of knowledge was available to remedy his current situation.

The fear and hate were almost too much to take, but a strange sense of wonder was present as well. While traveling through the memories a theme of love and joy kept coming to the front. This preacher had spent his entire life caring for others the way David had believed a religious person should, unlike Pastor Sinclair who cared for nothing other than himself. Pastor Stephens' memories contained thousands of acts of kindness toward any and all this man had come across in his many years. But what amazed David more was the memory of other religious leaders the pastor had befriended during his lifetime. They all put the needs of other people before their own, and although each dealt with personal flaws, the constant strive these men of faith had to better themselves was always present.

There were visions of comfort and consoling during times of tragedies where these leaders would spend hours upon hours with families trying to bring healing during troubled times. The tragedies were numerous, but the men of faith always kept a strong sense of pride and purpose which saw them through.

Stories of caring for youth were scattered amongst the memories too. A sense of importance to the younger generations was present, especially with those with unpleasant upbringings. Great care was taken to show that love and affection could help bring balance to the world of hate and discontent that they were accustomed to.

Another theme prevalent in the memory was the belief his host had in forgiveness and repentance. The religious leaders dealt with countless numbers of sinners both within the communities and their own congregations. Some of these men and women, according to the memories, had performed horrible acts of wrongdoing, but the preachers loved and cared for them as well. It was amazing at the amount of time and effort that was focused on the worst members of society and how a great multitude of those people were lead away from their wicked ways. The lives that this group turned around began to give David hope in his future, although that future was uncertain at the moment.

The travels through what was left of Pastor Stephens' mind were intriguing and enlightening, and David wanted to know more. He focused all of his effort into soaking up as much of the information available. There was little time before all energy left the body, but the speed of movement and absorption of knowledge happened at a rapid pace so not much time passed before David decided to make a change in the time remaining. It would seem to be a difficult task to set a new course for life, but it happened for David as quick as a light switch illuminates a room. The speed in which his mind was altered closely resembled the change he had made while suffering through the fire so many years ago. A sense of joy and purpose surrounded him which was welcomed after all the hate and anger that had been a part of his being for so long.

Back in the flames, the first task was to preserve his host's body the best he could. The pastor was gone, but there would inevitably be family left behind that would take comfort in having their loved one intact for burial. The fire was directed out of the room and held at bay. Although the ease of flame manipulation had increased since his first travels, fire extinguishment turned out to be a difficult task. The attempt at saving the church building would not be easy because of this fact, but all of David's concentration focused on slowing the spread which seemed to help. To his delight the fire was not harming Pastor Stephens' body, although after several minutes passed a concern crept up that eventually the fire would overtake everything. The ability to control an uncontrollable beast fell beyond his capabilities.

The time moved at a snail's pace, but a sense of value and triumph had enveloped him and seemed to make the task easier. How long he could hold on was not known, but just as the fire felt like it might break free from his grip, a mist began boiling up around him. David peered through the vapor and was delighted to see two firefighters crouching inside the front doors. The doors had been forced open, but his focus had been on controlling the fire and protecting the body. The firefighters' presence had not been detected until the water began to flow. A sense of relief followed, but not because of the possibility of getting a new host. The reassurance came from knowing that his wish of preserving the pastor and the church would come to fruition. Acquiring another host now went against what he had learned from Pastor Stephens so his concentration remained with keeping the flames from spreading as the water did its work.

The first firefighting team entered and cooled most of the fire. As the minutes ticked by others arrived to perform various tasks of extinguishment. While the flames decreased David could tell his energy was dissipating, but this did not concern him. A calm feeling encompassed his mind. He was unsure of what was happening, but he did not feel like the nothingness was coming back. Hours passed as the calmness increased and the awareness trailed off. The fire department was completing extinguishment and few embers remained. David's consciousness waned with every drop of water, and he realized that a new destination was on the horizon although there was no certainty where or what that might be. Wherever he found himself, David's one hope was that it would be a better place than he had been since the day of his death. That hope was still alive as a stream of liquid floated over the last pile of hot debris and the glow flickered then faded away.

Jake's first concern was Pastor Stephens. There was a chance that after the demon entered the fire, his host would be free to escape the church. That hope was dashed once the side corner of the building came into sight. If the pastor had survived the flames, which was unlikely, there were no doors or windows available to leave the building from that location. Jake could not risk the chance of getting burned by entering the church again so the only option left was to call in an alarm and wait for help to arrive. A major concern with that idea, however, was the danger of a responder becoming possessed so Jake's job would be to make sure everyone stayed in their gear the entire time. Some comfort came from the fact that the fire seemed to dissipate. He assumed that the demon was the cause, but he could not take any chances.

After the crews arrived and were updated on the situation, Jake took up a position next to his vehicle and watched until the final flame was extinguished. It took a few hours, but afterwards he relaxed knowing no one was injured and the threat was over. The fire would have to be investigated, especially with a fatality involved, but Jake was pleased and surprised by the crews' report of the good condition of the pastor. The body should have been burned beyond recognition with the amount of fire present, but there was little damage. At this point Jake was not going to question the strange occurrence. It would simply be a normal aspect of one of the demon fires. The smoke, on the other hand, had been too much for the lungs to bear and later the crime lab would determine that to be the cause of death.

Jake remained on the scene until Pastor Stephens' body was removed. After that he set up an engine crew to stage until his return. They knew he was exhausted from the last few days since the cabin fire so everyone agreed that he would go home and rest, although rest was not on his itinerary. During the drive home plans were made to help Chief Taylor and Firefighter Wade. The fact that both individuals were innocent was not a question anymore, but proving as much would be impossible. Jake was sure, however, that in speaking with the district attorney a compromise could be reached. Each church fire was deliberately set, but the fact that three unrelated perpetrators were involved would cause reasonable doubt in the minds of most jurors. Jake would make it clear that he lacked confidence in the cases and misdemeanor plea deals should be reached. The D.A. was a close friend, and although there would be pushback the plan would work. Each of the two living suspects would take first offender plea deals and after their sentences were complete, which should include little if any jail time, the records would be expunged. After that they should be able to continue their lives unencumbered. Of course neither one could continue their chosen careers locally, but Jake felt his plan would be a better result than each spending ten to twenty years in prison. It pained him to think that any negative outcomes would occur, but there was no other choice.

Jake pulled into his driveway as the sun peaked over the horizon. He rushed into the house heading straight for the bedroom. The bed looked tempting, and Jake knew that is where he should be, but he brushed past it and into the closet. He exited wearing exercise gear, placed a change of clothes in a gym back and off he went again. Several minutes later he passed the first entrance to the Kaleton Hill Trail. Sarah's car was there as predicted, but he did not stop, and instead drove further up the mountain. Close to the peak, he pulled into a parking space and scanned the area. As he focused a set of binoculars down the hill, he spotted a fluorescent green headband with ponytail trailing behind. Sarah was setting a brisk pace, and Jake knew that once he began his run, it would not take her long to catch up. He hoped after hearing his reason for standing her up she would be able to forgive, and he was eager to update her on all that had happened, but for now he just wanted to run alongside her and forget about all his worries for a while.

Chapter 13
A Burning Vengeance
(Epilogue 1)

Chris Cumbie

Demon Fire

The townsfolk were concerned about Rachel's wellbeing after the news of her son's demise spread. The normal reactions were expected and would have been understood. Inconsolable sobbing, deep depression, shunning friends or even lashing out at authority were responses that the community had braced itself for. To everyone's amazement, however, these reactions never came. What went on behind closed doors was anyone's guess, but the persona shown in public revealed only stoic grace.

After the devastating event, Rachel took a few days to herself and then she continued her work taking in laundry and helping with cleaning jobs. Everyone marveled at the way she bounced back from the tragedy, and after a while she even attended church again. First she would take part only in the activities and then after a while, the sermons. She would always sit near the front, and the congregation assumed that she had made peace with the consequences of her son's actions. Of course not many knew what those actions had been. Pastor Sinclair thought it best not to let the sordid details of his falsified charges leak out to the public. There would have been no way to release all the information without Rachel's name being sullied in the process, and since he still harbored a selfishly perverse desire, he wanted her to remain in the community. Banishment would have been easily accomplished, but keeping her close by with her reputation intact was the decision he made.

The first year post fire had been a worrisome one for the pastor. The burning death of David was more brutal than he ever would have imagined. The sight of his burning flesh and the blood-curdling screams haunted his dreams to the point that he swore the use of fire for an execution would never again occur. Another cause for concern dealt with Rachel herself. He did not trust that she seemed to cope so well with the situation, and he thought someday she might try to tell her story and set the community against him. The worry faded as time passed though and everything seemed to be as it was before the incident, although the pastor made it a point to keep at least some distance between him and Rachel.

As the second year was well underway, Rachel attended all church services and functions as she had fully acclimated back into the normal routine of life. Pastor Sinclair was thrilled with this outcome since his passion for her never abated, and as the time passed, he thought her adjusting so well after the tragedy must be due to her obvious passion for him. This narcissistic view so engulfed him that before long he thought about testing his theory by inviting her to a counseling session. An outlandish notion, but one he believed might be worth a try.

He felt that a group session might ease her back into the process, and to the pastor's joy Rachel agreed to attend. The meeting went well, and feedback from the attendees was positive. Bolstered by these results, more meetings were set as the invitees dwindled down to where only a few came to each meeting. Rachel of course always received an invitation, and she was more than willing to take part in the discussions. The interactions between her and the pastor were always cordial, and at times flirtatious, although at that time he was still seeing to it that the two of them were never alone together.

As the second year was winding down, the pastor became bold enough to ask to begin one-on-one counseling sessions again. Trepidation arose again as he feared that bringing her into the same situation that precipitated the tragedy of the past might stir up emotions in her that could interfere with his grand scheme, but his desire was too great not to at least try.

The first meeting began awkwardly. The pastor was on edge, and for one of the few times in his life he was not sure what to say or how to proceed. The next few meetings seemed to go well, however, with playful banter prevalent in their interactions. The meetings went so well that the next step was to hold a session in a more personal setting, and Rachel was invited to the pastor's residence to partake in another private counseling. He made it known that the session would be less formal and that a meal would be served. Few options for fashion wear were available, but Rachel had gone to great lengths to make her ordinary clothes into something to show off her toned body. As she gazed at herself in the cracked mirror hanging in the bedroom, she turned and admired the wonderful job she had done with the outfit.

After a twirl to check the back, her eyes lifted once more to her face. Rachel had not cried for some time. After David died, she locked herself in the house and sobbed for what seemed like days. The crying had been so violent that her throat and head throbbed long after the tears dissipated. Over the past year the emotions had been kept in check by placing defense mechanisms in her mind and hardening her heart to the pain she felt. Now as she critiqued the face looking back at her in the reflection a single tear rolled down her cheek. It was the last tear she would shed for a long time.

Demon Fire

Pastor Sinclair opened the door and became weak in the knees. His boisterous tales of travel contained more fiction than fact. He had never visited the streets of London nor floated the canals of Venice, but he had been many more places and experienced more things than anyone in Haniford ever had, and in all of his travels there had never been a time when his eyes had found as much beauty as stood before him now.

Religion had never been something the pastor had given his heart to. The church had always been more of a tool used to build himself up rather than an institution he held dear to his heart. The idea of his superiority was real to him, but until now it could not be attributed to any sort of divine intervention, but seeing Rachel standing before him alone in his house after all he had taken from her made him think that maybe his greatness was not based solely on his brilliant mind and cunning nature. Maybe it was truly a higher power that shined grace down upon him.

This idea became reinforced as he pulled Rachel to him and passionately kissed her. To his elation he found that he was being kissed back with just as much passion. He knew at that point he was right. He was truly blessed with a power over people's hearts, minds and possibly even their souls. What he could accomplish with this new found potential would be limited only by his imagination.

The rush of excitement between having his conquest and realizing his greatness made him almost oblivious to the discomfort. Pain was certainly present, but the pastor was blind to its cause. His attention remained on the kiss and what it meant to him and his position in life, and as the two pairs of lips parted, the pastor opened his eyes. His face was flush with excitement, and he could not hide the exuberant emotions that permeated through him. The discomfort had worsened though, and it began to wrestle his attention away from the fantasy. His eyes focused for a moment on Rachel's face. Her expression had turned from soft and subtle to stoic and uncaring. This puzzled the pastor until his sight shifted downward and fell upon the blood soaked blade.

The first strike had been a quick thrust into the abdomen. The second came as the pastor looked back up with his jaw open in disbelief. The blade had an upward angle this time and found a space just below the rib cage. As she had practiced alone in her home for months, the blade was pulled back again, flipped and thrust forward as the hand grasped the handle once more this time coming down from above and entering the neck just above the sternum. The blade was again removed as Rachel stepped back into the night air. The pastor fell to the floor with a thud as she looked down on him. She felt neither hate nor sorrow, and she did not allow herself to care for his suffering one way or the other. There was no need for pleasure or pain on her part. Justice was cold and impartial as was the new woman standing before the heap of death splayed out before her.

Constable Matthews entered Cyrus' bedroom and bowed his head as a show of respect to the community elder. The room was poorly lit, but the look of a man being chased by death still shown through the candlelight. Cyrus had fallen ill several months prior and whatever had caught hold of him would not let go until he was conquered. After the greetings, the constable held out the item he had brought with him wrapped in cloth. Cyrus motioned in the direction of a small table in the corner and it was brought over and the item placed on top. As the cloth peeled away a glimmer of steel could be seen as the bed pillows were readjusted to give a better angle for viewing.

"What do we have here?" The blade of the knife was approximately six inches long and had a polished wooden handle which was nothing like the two had ever seen before. The knives familiar to them were normally working tools which were long and wide with worn out blades from over-sharpening. This piece had been well made and honed to a fine point. There were darkened areas on both the blade and handle that looked to Cyrus as though it might be dried blood. His eyesight, unlike the rest of his body, was not failing him.

"This is the knife Rachel brought to me after stabbing Pastor Sinclair to death."

Cyrus was shocked. He lay back in bed and thought for a moment. "Tell me the details constable."

"Well, she came to my office not much over two and a half hours ago. She just opened the door, walked right in and set this down on my desk. Said she stabbed the pastor then told me to go check his house. It was the darndest thing I had ever seen I tell you. She was standing there all made up. I have never seen Rachel look so pretty, but her clothes were bloodstained and then this knife. I didn't know what to think. I called for Joseph and all three of us went to the church. Sure enough Pastor Sinclair was laying there dead on his doorstep. Stabbed in at least two or three different places. There was blood everywhere. I've got her locked up in the shack with Joseph standing guard. Well, I wouldn't really call it standing guard. He's watching from the outside. I think he's plumb scared to death of her, and I don't blame him. Rachel has changed. She's got this look to her. Kinda stone cold, and the way she talked about what happened. She gave us all the details with no sign of caring that she had killed someone.

Cyrus looked away and leaned back into the bed. A long sigh was followed by his scratchy voice. "This proves it."

"Proves what?" Asked Constable Matthews.

Demon Fire

"It proves the story young David told me about the incident that began this entire chain of events. This was a revenge killing constable. A brutal, well designed and thought out payback. The lack of emotion shows she has no remorse for what she had done. Her conscious is clear. The reason is that Pastor Sinclair really did attack her in the way David had described before and then burned the only family she had left to cover up the truth." Cyrus paused as he gasped for air. His lungs did not have the strength for long periods of conversation anymore. David's story had been relayed to the constable by Cyrus a short time after the burning. The tale was told in passing, and neither one believed it to be true at the time.

"Do you really think that?" The constable asked after Cyrus was able to slow his breathing.

"I have no doubt. I have never felt comfortable with the way this whole thing played out, and it's just as much our fault as the pastor's. We did nothing to question or interfere. We merely sat there and let it happen, and even though we both believed Pastor Sinclair's version, there is no way we should have let that boy burn."

"So what do you suggest we do? I mean, I understand what you are saying, but she killed the pastor. We have to do something."

Another several deep breaths as Cyrus garnered the strength to speak again.

"The penalty for murder is hanging. Although this is not a true murder, and no one would approve of that outcome. Part of me thinks she was justified for doing what she did, but that does not mean the townsfolk will approve. So that leaves us only one option. She must leave and never return."

Cyrus, despite his advanced age and poor health, was still one of the wisest men in the community. With the pastor dead the important decisions of the town fell to the constable, but his limited intelligence and lack of ambition were not the attributes of a good leader. He was happy to follow the advice of Cyrus on the case of what to do with Rachel, and he went back for consultation many times on various issues after that. This working relationship proved to be helpful until the inevitable passing. After Cyrus' death the town's business was handled haphazardly and with poor results. The area's population fluctuated over the years, but the structure of the community diminished and the town of Haniford eventually faded away.

Rachel was formally banished from the area and once gone; she never came back, although years later outsiders began telling stories as they would pass through town. The stories were of an amazing woman who would stand up to any man in a knife fight. This woman traveled both near and far, at times working for the law and at times working against it if need be. When the stories were told, the woman's exquisite beauty was always mentioned as well as her uncaring attitude when it came to killing those who had caused harm to others. The response from the community upon hearing the tales was always positive, even to the point that they wished a female hero like that might one day live amongst them.

Chris Cumbie

Chapter 14

Embers

(Epilogue 2)

Chris Cumbie

Demon Fire

Isaiah James and his girlfriend Amy Cuthbert pulled to the edge of the wood line on a cool autumn evening. The two had been dating for a few months, and this weekend trip across the border into Kentucky was to be their first overnight getaway. An old abandoned house could be seen through the trees, and it looked even spookier than the pictures. The inside would be explored later as the darkness deepened, but for now they had other plans. A snuggle by the campfire followed by some much anticipated tent time was foremost on their minds.

The site seemed perfect for camping with a long open field and plenty of downed logs and limbs for firewood. Not to mention the supposedly haunted house with trees growing out of the top of it located a hundred feet away. The two of them were thrill seekers that loved to be scared so the thought of spending the night in this environment seemed ideal. The tale they had heard was that the two-story residence had been occupied by a cult fifty or sixty years ago and the members would hold rituals involving sacrifice by fire. Spirits of those who had passed were said to inhabit the area and especially the house. This was what the couple had hoped for. They wanted to have a good fright, and ghosts hanging around an old rundown house in the middle of nowhere was more than they could have dreamed. The exploration would have to wait for now, however, as a chill set in with the setting sun.

When Isaiah brought the first armful of wood over he saw that Amy had nearly completed the tent. Knowing Amy was showing off her expertise at camping, he decided that a roaring fire would be needed to put him on a level playing field. To this end Isaiah began his work. First a layer of dried leaves and tiny twigs were placed inside a circle of rocks he had set up. Above this he stacked a layer of bigger sticks placed in a way that plenty of air would travel through. On the top, the larger pieces of wood were arranged. With everything ready, he brought out the tool which every good camper should never leave home without - a lighter.

Although Isaiah was new at the camping lifestyle a few internet searches had at least taught him how to start a fire, but he was surprised at the speed this task had been accomplished. From the moment the flame touched the first twig the fire grew quickly. The larger pieces of wood, which are supposed to take longer to catch, flamed up right before his eyes. The growth of the fire was noticed by Amy as well, but it was just an afterthought to both. A couple in love did not pay much attention to such trivial things.

Isaiah and Amy had decided to forgo the tent and set up their bedding as close to the campfire as possible. The main portion of wood had dwindled down and only a bed of hot coals remained. A reddish glow from these embers was just enough to silhouette their bodies against the backdrop of the night. The love they made was full of joy, happiness and caring. These were all the emotions that would be expected in their situation although one feeling that was present seemed to be out of place. This wayward emotion was fear. Fear of being ignored. Fear of being left behind. A fear that had lain dormant, watching and waiting. Waiting for the moment to arrive. Waiting for an unsuspecting couple. Waiting for a spark. Waiting for an oversized sleeping bag to be placed a little too close. Waiting for an opening. Waiting for an exposed piece of flesh. Waiting...

"Crap!"

"What is it? What happened?"

Isaiah jumped up and quickly turned his back so Amy could see.

"Ouch." Amy said. "That looks painful." A blister was already forming on Isaiah's thigh.

"It'll be okay." Isaiah said, trying to put on a brave face. "It's just a little burn. I guess one of the hot coals popped out and got me."

"Looks like it." Amy said as she took her shoe and brushed the burning red ember back into the fire. "No need to worry though. If that's the worst thing that happens to us this weekend, I think we'll be just fine."

The End

Author's Note

I would like to thank you for reading my book. A great deal of time and effort went in to the writing, editing and publishing of this story, and I hope I was able to make it enjoyable.

If you liked this book, please visit my Amazon book page and leave a review.

This is my first novel. Maybe one day there will be another.

Chris Cumbie

Demon Fire

Chris Cumbie

Made in the USA
Columbia, SC
26 February 2019